MW01030134

THE BEMA

THE BEMA

A *Story about the*
Judgment Seat of Christ

Tim Stevenson

Fair Havens Publications®
Gainesville, Texas

Design and production by Merrikay Lee, Lee Publishing Services, Inc., Highland Village, Texas.

ISBN 0-9664803-1-7

Printed in the United States of America

Fair Havens Publications®
P. O. Box 1238
Gainesville, Texas 76241-1238

Web Site: www.fairhavenspub.com

To the six people who make me a rich man:
my wife, Deb, and our children,
Katie, Matt, Liz, Meredith, and Daniel.

Tim Stevenson is the Senior Pastor of Crossroads Bible Church in Bartonville, Texas, north of Dallas-Fort Worth. He has served in that capacity since 1993.

After graduating from Southern Methodist University in 1976, he served with Discipleship Counseling Services from 1978-1990 (as Vice-President for the last eight years), and as Executive Director of the Christian Concern Foundation of Dallas from 1991-1993.

Tim has maintained an active teaching ministry throughout his years in vocational Christian work, including seminars, conferences, radio programs, and discipleship training. He has also written various literature on Christian living, and produced several audiotape series. Some of his recent sermons can be heard on the Internet by visiting the Crossroads Bible Church Web site: www.crossroadsbible.org.

He and his wife, Deb, live in Flower Mound, Texas, with their five children, Katie, Matt, Liz, Meredith, and Daniel.

John Cook is the professional artist who painted the picture used for the book cover. He left a successful career as a commercial illustrator to pursue the fine arts. He applies a diverse visual interest to a diversity of subject areas, including still life, portraits, animals, modern cowboys, as well as landscapes and waterscapes. Recently, he traveled to London and Paris to produce a series of street scenes. His clients include major corporations such as American Airlines, CBS Broadcasting, Neiman-Marcus, Disney Epcot Center, Frito-Lay, Hilton Hotels, and Shell Oil.

He and his wife, Jean, are active members of Crossroads Bible Church. They have two young-adult children. His e-mail address is heresjohnny101@msn.com.

FOREWORD

⌇

Ever so often you find a story that strikes a chord. Reading Dickens' unparalleled tale of substitution, *A Tale of Two Cities,* my heart raced with my fingers as I turned the climactic pages. I've traveled with Steinbeck as he and his dog Charley introduced me to people I'd never meet, in towns I'd never see. I remember reading *Watership Down* as a teenager, falling in love with the misplaced cottontails as they searched for home. Sitting in the balcony, looking at the stage though binoculars, I wept during the final thirty minutes of *Les Miserables,* as the power of grace demonstrated in story form swept through my senses and left me stunned.

Tim Stevenson would never claim to be Dickens, Steinbeck, or Victor Hugo, but he has written a story from his heart so powerful you will want to read it in one sitting. Musrasaki Shikibu said that the art of the novel is more than an author just recounting someone else's adventures.

It results from the author's own experiences that move him
to such passion, he cannot contain it in his heart.

Tim can't keep this story in. After you read it you
won't be able to either. I set the book down and immediately started planning a dramatic presentation for my
church. On two Sunday mornings, I transported my people from their frantic temporality to the Bema: a place few
had heard of, a final chapter full of suspense and thrills.
Since that time, the tapes of that presentation have been
duplicated time and again, the story being told, and lives
being changed.

Some of you will be mesmerized by this book, discovering a biblical theology never before recognized. Others
will be reminded in a fresh way that living for today can be
hazardous, but living for THE Day...now that's another
story!

Pete Briscoe
Senior Pastor
Bent Tree Bible Fellowship
Carrollton, Texas

Preface

⟋

This book has had a most unusual journey from conception to birth. The original idea came to me suddenly and unsought one evening in 1990, but more than eight years intervened before the first words were written. It was always "the story I'm going to write down sometime." Once begun, it emerged rapidly and easily in only five months. The rest was the hard work of rewriting and polishing.

There are many people I would like to thank for their helpful input and encouragement:

Pete Briscoe, who read the manuscript just after the first draft was completed, and responded with enthusiasm. It was Pete who immediately saw the dramatic possibilities in the story, which has opened up avenues I never imagined. It now seems *The Bema* will have a thriving ministry as a drama in addition to the novel.

Sherry Alpert, Nancy Gundlach, Kim Kerr, and Edna McDaniel, the wonderful ladies who serve in our church's office. Reading the story virtually as it emerged from the printer, they reacted as if it were an old Saturday afternoon serial. As each chapter ended in a cliffhanger, their demands for more spurred me on.

J. Ray and Joan Smith, my publishers, for sharing my vision and commitment for this story, and for their diligent and loving editing.

Paul Floyd, for his insights from a businessman's experience.

Mike Farney, who knows well the highest levels of the computer software business, and offered helpful suggestions.

Chris and Alice Morgan, for stepping forward to help make this book a reality.

My fellow pastors at Crossroads: Dave Semmelbeck, Neil Curran, Brent McKinney, Mike Messerli, and Bob Blassingame. Their friendship and fellowship in the gospel make it a joy to serve together. Also, my fellow Elders, who allow me the freedom to write.

Dr. Henry Brandt, one of my heroes in the ministry, for his friendship, encouragement, and example.

John Cook, for contributing his outstanding talent as an artist.

Merrikay Lee, for her sensitive and helpful editing and production work.

David Dolan, Gary Terashita, Bob Ross, Jamie Lash, Greg Clouse, and many others who spoke highly of the book and encouraged me to keep going.

Thanks to you all for your encouragement, friendship, and love.

May you live for The Day!

Tim Stevenson
Flower Mound, Texas
June 29, 2000

CHAPTER 1

✧

The piercing shriek of the alarm clock jolted me. Disoriented, I rose to my elbows, looking around in bewilderment. A few seconds later, I groaned and slapped the off button with disgust. How could Monday morning be here so soon?

I knew it was irrational, but I sneered in futile defiance at the digital glow reading 4:55 as I got up. This day was beginning just like hundreds of other days had begun. There was no hint that my life was about to change forever.

A glance at Susan sleeping soundly increased my irritation. Not that she didn't work hard at her job and as a mother, too. It was just the natural resentment the earlier riser feels toward the one who gets to sleep a little longer.

Three hours of sleep is not enough! I was waking up quickly, though, despite having worked late into the night. This will be a big day! I thought as I showered.

Aren't they all? Asked a small ironic voice in the back of my mind.

Ignoring it, I began to preview the day's events. Most important would be a meeting with a major client. If we can close the Wiederman deal, I … I mean we … will make a killing! And, yes, I will finally get my fair share. After all, I have worked on this project for months, and I deserve it as much … more than anyone else in the office! I snorted slightly. The partners always manage to get their cut, whether they've earned it or not. But one of these days, I'll be in their position, and I'll be making two to three times as much as I do now. I'll show them how to manage that place!

How much money do you need to make? the voice whispered again.

All right, I know money isn't everything. After all, I am a Christian, and I've tried to live a good life. I go to church faithfully … most of the time anyway. Yes, I know I haven't been involved like I used to be. I know I haven't opened a Bible in a long while. I just don't have the time I used to have. Making a living takes everything I've got, and I'm good at what I do! I have a reputation for quality work and dependability. I'm ethical and honest!

At that thought, I felt a clenching in my stomach and something like a weight on my shoulders. I knew what it was, because I had felt it often—ever since that time more than a year before when I let myself slip. For the first time, I had knowingly and deliberately stepped over a line I prided myself on never crossing. Beforehand, I told myself it was a small step, hardly worth noticing. Afterward, it felt like a dagger to the heart.

For weeks I had wrestled with the guilt. "It was nothing more than anyone else would have done in my place." "Any fair-minded person would have understood my position." "My action was legal, and it would, without question, stand up in court." So had my internal defense attorney argued. The part of my heart which was once spiritually sensitive and ethically firm continued to sound an alarm. But by now, my reactions were so well trained by months of rationalizing and defending myself against myself that it was no longer necessary to go through the arguments. I could turn away from the guilt feelings as easily as closing a closet door. This time the voice did not reply. It had all been said.

But aren't Christians supposed to work hard? Isn't that why they call it the Protestant work ethic? Isn't hard work what built this great country and gave us all these blessings? What could be more important than achieving all I can achieve in life?

That was a major misstep. Before I could complete the question in my mind, the faces of my three children flashed before me. There was a time when my wife and children were the most important things in my life, second only to the Lord himself. My heart sank and my hand holding the razor fell to the counter top. I looked into my own eyes in the mirror for the first time. I heard eight year-old Janie's voice, saying, "When are you coming home, Daddy? Can you come to Open House at school tonight?" I had mumbled a noncommittal reply as Susan's eyes searched mine. I heard ten year-old Mark ask, "Can you come to my game tomorrow night?" "I don't know, we'll see," I had lied to him, knowing that I would be working late, as usual. Last Wednesday, after I pulled into the driveway and got out of my car, I was met by five year-old Jeffrey. With a happy grin he said, "What are you doing home, Daddy? It's not dark yet." Searching my reflection, I whispered, "Dan Mathewson, what's happened to you?"

My defenses rallied. I know I work a lot. But it's them I'm working for! This beautiful house (and maybe an even bigger one in that exciting new neighborhood north of town) is possible because of my work. The kids go to good schools. They have good clothes. Susan is well dressed and drives a nice car, too. She wouldn't like it if we were living less well! Because of what I do, and I suppose somewhat because of what she brings in from her job, we're able to support this lifestyle.

O really? said the voice. *What about those hints she has made about feeling terribly sad because she is not there when the kids come home from school? About how she would love to be a full-time Mom? That she wouldn't mind wearing budget clothes if it meant more time at home?*

This was getting tiresome. I dressed and went to the car.

I'm really sick of this freeway, I thought. Even leaving early enough to miss the worst of the traffic doesn't make it enjoyable. People seem to drive even crazier at 5:30 in the morning, maybe because they're afraid of getting caught in the later morning rush.

Even before thinking about the big afternoon meeting, there was another unpleasant item on my schedule. I've really had it with Mary Lou! She used to perform well, but she isn't cutting it lately. She looks tired all the time, she doesn't contribute much useful in our planning sessions, and I'm tired of carrying her end of the load along with mine. Her production is way down.

There may be a reason for that, you know. The voice hadn't stayed at home. *She has a sick child, and has been under severe personal pressure for months. Don't you recall her little comments that made you wonder if she and her husband might be having trouble? Sustained stress can be tough on marriages.*

But that's not my problem, I answered. In the real world, performance is everything. Excuses are for losers. Hogan wouldn't cut me any slack if production fell off, you can be sure of that! This is the real world we're talking about, not a charity!

Suddenly a flash and a surge of paralyzing, electric fear interrupted my thoughts. A black BMW had come flying across two lanes to squeeze into the tiny gap between my car and the one ahead. It changed lanes again to the right through another small space and raced ahead at a speed far above the seventy-three miles per hour of the traffic flow. The objective danger had passed even before I could grasp the facts of the situation, but my anger was only beginning. Cursing the driver, I wished to get my hands on him. I could see myself slamming my car into his—not only for the stupidity of his actions, but also for his arrogance. I knew he was laughing at the rest of us, and my anger burned higher. My foot flexed to floor the gas pedal and go charging after the BMW, though I didn't know what I would do if I caught up to him. Then I realized I was hemmed in by traffic with no way out. I cursed the driver and his mother, and backed off the gas.

It took me the rest of the morning drive to forget about the highway insult, but my pulse finally calmed. I parked in the garage and walked to our building. Pushing through the revolving door, I headed for the elevator, hoping to escape notice. No such luck. I heard a booming voice say cheerfully, "Good morning, Mr. Mathewson! How are you today?" This happens every day.

I smiled weakly, and replied, "Pretty well, Joe." I didn't feel like it, but I added, "And how are you?"

Joe (whose last name I can't recall) said, "Can't complain. No, I can't complain. The Lord is good to me every day. 'If ye then, being evil, know how to give good gifts unto your children, how much more shall your Father which is in heaven give good things to them that ask him?' Has he been good to you, Mr. Mathewson?"

Joe the security guard (in fact, "Thesecurityguard" may as well have been his last name—it was the only name I ever attached to him) was a rail-thin African-American seemingly in his sixties, though it was impossible to tell. He could easily have been ten years older or younger. He lacked much education, judging by his usual conversation. There was no missing his knowledge of the Bible, though. Even in short encounters, he liberally sprinkled Bible verses quoted from memory. Joe was likable enough in his way, but his sunny personality in the morning was sometimes hard to take. And Joe had an irritating tendency to ask embarrassing questions, like the last one.

Has God been good to me? I haven't thought about that in a while. "Yeah, I guess so," I replied without spirit.

"I'm glad to hear it, glad to hear it," he said as he presented me to the elevator. His personal interest made it feel almost like being dropped off at the nursery school door by my mother. "Well, sir, I hope you have a great day!"

The elevator door closed and I pushed the button for the twenty-seventh floor.

CHAPTER 2

I stepped out of the elevator onto the plush carpet outside the office suites of Hogan, Jeter & White. Approaching the main door, I saw that it stood open, the way blocked by a wheeled trash bin. I pushed it aside and entered.

"I'm very sorry, sir," gushed a Spanish-tinged voice. "I was just finishing up." A short, plump woman dressed in an industrial blue work uniform peered around the corner.

"That's okay. No problem," I answered numbly, walking to my office. The key was in my hand, but, again, the door stood open. Putting my briefcase on the credenza, I sat down at the desk and pulled out a stack of papers. My stomach was already churning acid in anticipation of our big presentation that afternoon. I really wanted to nail the Wiederman deal.

"Would you like some coffee?" said a voice. The cleaning woman was leaning inside the office door. "I started it a little while ago, since I know you like to come in early." I grunted affirmatively, and she scurried off. Returning with a large mug, she set it down at my right hand.

"How are your wife and babies?" she asked.

Slightly annoyed at her interruptions, I smiled weakly and said without taking my eyes off the reports, "Oh, everybody's fine."

"They're so beautiful!" the lady said enthusiastically, beaming at the family portrait she held. I looked up. What was this lady's name? *Juanita* her name tag read.

My concentration finally broken, I softened a little and looked at her directly for the first time. "Yes. They are, aren't they? Thanks for saying so."

"There is nothing more important than family," she went on. "I miss my husband so much since he died. My children are all grown and live in different places. All except Gloria, who's eighteen. She'll go to college at Tech next fall. I have four children and seven grandchildren, but I don't get to see them as much as I would like to. Did I ever tell you about my husband? Carlos was killed in an accident at work."

This was really more than I wanted to know about Juanita. I mumbled a sympathetic word and half-listened as she described her husband's death—evidently some kind of construction accident. I looked at her with a concerned expression while I wondered how much longer it would be before I could get back to my real concerns.

"Well, I have to go," Juanita said. "I have to take Gloria to school and go to work." I must have looked blankly puzzled, because she added, "I work from nine to one as a receptionist in a small law office. I have lots of bills and a college education to pay for."

The woman finally prepared to leave. She paused at the door and turned. "I pray for you every night while I work, Mr. Mathewson. You are a good man, and you have a wonderful family. Good-bye."

Finally! Looking back at the papers in front of me, I realized the need to run some figures. I opened the second right-hand drawer to get my calculator. I'm not exactly a clean-desk executive, so there was a mess of pens, reports, and miscellaneous items inside. Moving an envelope aside, my eyes fell on a Bible. I paused, looking at it, then picked it up. I held it before me without opening it. Things sure have changed, I thought.

Do you remember when the best part of your day was the first hour? That quiet voice in the back of my mind sounded friendlier as it reminded me of a happy time.

Yes. Just a few years ago, my routine was simple and regular: arrive early enough at the office to have some uninterrupted time for personal preparation. I used to love beginning my work day by reading the Scriptures. Of course, I had more time and much less pressure at my old company, before coming to Hogan, Jeter & White. There was real pleasure then in feeding myself on the Word of God and getting my head screwed on straight before taking on work and the world.

That's because man doesn't live by bread alone. You used to know that.

Times change. I found work exciting, and discovered that I was good at this business. There were glowing accolades and financial rewards. By starting work earlier, I found I was more productive.

You mean financially more productive, of course.

Well, yeah. I got a head-start on the competition. It began to feel like I was wasting prime time doing my devotions.

Interesting phrase: "Doing my devotions." Once it was "spending time with the Lord" that was most important to you. "Doing devotions" is a far cry from enjoying a relationship. No wonder it didn't feel like a great loss when you gave it up altogether.

I didn't feel like arguing anymore, but I couldn't resist mustering one more defense. Look. I've been in all kinds of Bible study groups and classes over the years, and I know the Bible pretty well, even if I quit doing my morning ritual. It doesn't really matter when I study, does it? I just found that I got a much faster start at work if I jumped right in. I was better prepared.

But you were not better prepared spiritually or morally. Do you think it was accidental that you began to slip ethically not long after?

I'd had enough debate. To quiet the voice, I put the Bible back in the drawer and shut it. I focused my attention on the stack of reports and thought about the Wiederman deal for the next ninety minutes.

"Well, are you ready to perform?" said an even voice from my office doorway. I was more internally startled than I showed, but I was practiced at controlling my exterior. Something in me always seemed to jump at the first sound of Derek Hogan's voice, though nothing on his surface accounted for my reaction. He was considered an extremely handsome man—jet-black hair, prominent dark eyebrows, sharp even features, and a straight smile revealing perfect teeth. Always impeccably dressed, he moved in the highest social circles in our city. Known as a powerful mover and shaker from circles of commerce to the symphony association to his country club. Everything he touched made scads of money, including our present company.

But I cannot say that I liked him. Why not? I guess the most honest answer is that I was afraid of him. Derek Hogan was dangerous, and never more dangerous than when he was smiling. Just like a shark. He tolerated me because I made him a lot of money, and I worked for him because he gave me the chance to make a lot of money. Somehow, nonverbally, his smile and handshake in congratulation of a success also communicated a near death threat for future failure.

"Yes, I'm ready," I replied evenly and firmly. You learned quickly never to answer in anything but positively confident terms to Hogan. If you were to drag your feet, whine, hedge your answers, or plead for more time, you would receive a withering stare and a sneer and earn the description, slug, meaning weakling. You would get the same response if you were not willing to put in the excessive hours he expected, regardless of your performance. It didn't matter if you got the job done in fewer hours. If you left the office early (which to Hogan meant any time that got me home before the kids went to bed), you, too, were a slug. And slugs had no place in his company. They were to be squished underfoot.

In my case, however, I had the track record and position that allowed me to raise questions. Something in the reports I had been reading bothered me.

"Derek, there is one thing that's concerning me a little," I said. He stared at me, unsmiling. "Our software jockeys have been working frantically to get these programs finished. It looks like they've made it, but the software hasn't been Beta tested yet. There's a pile of data and research, but they just got it to me, and I haven't had a chance to review it and make sure it will do what we say. They *say* it will, but I'm not so sure. Plus, Wiederman is going to ask about documentation and tech support. I don't think we have anybody who knows enough to actually do it. Training, support, and service will be written in the contract."

Hogan stared down where he was slowly picking at his thumbnails. He looked up at me, still without expression, and said nothing. His eyes were ominously dark.

"Derek, I'm going to be delivering this presentation." At your insistence, I thought, but didn't say. "I'll be the one giving them my word about the great quality of this product, which I do believe. But when it comes to testing data or tech support, what am I supposed to say?"

Hogan stared at me for a moment, then smiled. "That's why we have you in this position, Mathewson. Because, besides me, you're the best deal maker we have. Do you think I'd ever trust Baker with something like this? The man's an idiot! He's there to talk about bits and bytes and sound technical enough to relax them. You're the point man for us."

As much as I hate to admit it, having Derek Hogan call me his "best deal maker" and refer to me as his "point man" caused a warm glow of pleasure to wash over me. He didn't compliment many people about anything.

Hogan paced, waving his arms a bit for emphasis. "Tech support is all bull, anyway. Companies today have their own IT departments. Wiederman will modify our package and personalize it before the year's out. They'll figure out for themselves how to do what they want to do. They all do the same thing. Those technical support clauses are just a license to whine. They'll screw up the program, then they'll call *us* and blame *us* for its failure. The lawyers always have to clean it up afterward, no matter *what* we tell them up front." He didn't need to mention that he had a team of lawyers under the leadership of Ed White who probably could have gotten Hitler off the hook.

Hogan sat on the edge of my desk, looking fatherly all of a sudden. "Dan, I'm for ethics in business, but let's get real. Business is war. Nobody is obligated on a battlefield to notify the enemy what his next move is."

I merely looked at him without responding. I couldn't really argue with him, but I didn't feel right about his reasoning, either.

"Dan, do you remember when I first hired you? Our first meeting together was over lunch. I told you then my operating philosophy. Do you remember what I told you?"

I remembered. "Bucks is the name of the game," I said.

He nodded. "Bucks is still the name of the game. It's the only reason we play, and the way we keep score. And if bucks is how we keep score, score big! You've got a chance to make more than you ever dreamed. Enough to do whatever fool thing it is you want to do. *If* you don't get stupid."

Hogan paused, then continued. "I never told you this, but it was Jack Beeler himself who recommended you to me. He told me you had real potential, and he was right. That's why I hired you away from that loser outfit you were with. If you keep performing around here, you'll really be in the driver's seat one of these days. This deal alone may get you a partner's share."

My head swam at the suggestion. *A partner!* Yes, I'd thought about it as a future possibility, but not anytime soon. That could set me up to make millions! And the former mayor, Jack Beeler, recommended me to Hogan? My imagination started to wander. I felt hardly a sting when my former co-workers and friends, a group of honest, talented people, were called "losers."

Hogan brought me back by slapping my desk. "You're either on the team, or you're not! Think about it! And be ready to do your job at two o'clock this afternoon." He briskly walked out of my office.

CHAPTER 3

֍

I spent the next hour looking over reports and calculating how I was going to get Wiederman to buy the deal. It was no mystery why Hogan was so interested: it meant millions to our company and to him. Why it was so important that I be the point man, though, I still couldn't figure. It would be nice to believe that I was really his best deal maker, but I couldn't truly buy it. Hogan was always working an angle. He never wasted effort.

I took another look at the contract. As it was drawn up, I seemed to be omnipresent. My signature as representative of Hogan, Jeter & White would be on practically every other page. I would be the face man, the negotiator, the representative. Yes, I've done a lot of productive work for our company in the past, but how have I suddenly become so prominent? My ego didn't like to admit it, but down deep I knew I wasn't that important—at least not yet.

"You wanted to see me?" said a voice, interrupting me. Gerald Baker, a large and friendly bear-like man, sat down

in the chair before my desk. As senior partner in the software division, Baker was my superior in the organizational
structure, but he seldom acted like it. He was the chief
technoid over the other technoids, and he thought about
little beyond the technical sphere. He treated me like an
equal, and sometimes—especially in regard to the business
side of things—like a superior. "You worried about our big
meeting?" he asked.

"No, I'm not worried," I lied. "I know you tech guys
have been working your tails off to get this thing ready…"
I paused. "Gerry, it just doesn't look ready to me."

Baker didn't appear upset. He sniffed, and said, "It's
mostly ready. And I think it's pretty good. Besides, if programs had to be totally bug-free, there'd be no software
sold anywhere in the world."

"I can understand that," I answered, "but this deal is
much more than that. Wiederman's entire manufacturing
and distribution business will be working off it. And we'll
have a whole set of contractual guarantees, obligations,
and promises of tech support. If it hasn't been Beta tested
yet, how do we know we can live up to the agreement?"

Baker shrugged. "You got me. Look, Mathewson, this
won't be the first time we've flown by the seat of our pants.
We're wheelers and dealers. When you work for Derek
Hogan, you learn to do business on the fly. We collect our
money up front and worry about what happens later.
Chances are, we'll have the bugs figured out before anything blows up. But even if we don't, we can string them
out for months until we can solve it or until they give up.
Either way, we've got the money."

I didn't like either of those options. I frowned in
thought.

Baker laughed. "Jeez, Dan, don't you know why you're the point man on this? It's because old Henry loves you! You could sell him swamp land in Florida."

I *really* didn't like the sound of that, but I knew immediately what he meant. Henry Wiederman was a business leader of the old school. Seventy years old or more. One of that generation who began doing blue-collar work and retained that spirit even after owning and operating his own business for years—did deals with a handshake. A crusty, honest businessman, a deacon in his church. Treated his employees with integrity and loyalty of a day gone by. A dinosaur.

And "old Henry" did like me. I had met him through some of my father's acquaintances when I was just starting out, and he had given me some consulting work. We had crossed paths several times over the years, and—here was the bottom line—he trusted me.

That afternoon, I was supposed to look Henry Wiederman in the eye and tell him that our software is the best available for his business, that it will do all we said it will do, and that we will back up all the promises in the contract. And I would sign every line on behalf of Hogan, Jeter & White. In truth, it would really be my word on every line.

"Is that all?" Baker asked, rising to leave, "because I've got lots to do before two o'clock." I nodded and he exited the room.

Mary Lou Bernet now sat before my desk. Her eyes were red and tired, and she looked drained. Quite a change from the dynamo she had once been. I could have used her help preparing for the Wiederman deal, but she had been basically useless. She had a two year-old child chronically sick with some disorder I can't pronounce. A little time off is one thing, I thought, but this is ridiculous. Even when she's here, she isn't *here.*

Come on now! said my other mind. *Business is not everything. What if it were your own child who was sick? Is there no place for compassion and mercy in your mad rush for bucks?*

The voice struck clearer notes than in any of my other inner debates. I did feel sorry for her. But right at the point of giving in to those feelings, I was reminded of the intense pressure I was under to produce and perform. Mary Lou's troubles were going to increase the weight on me.

These were not new thoughts, and they only took a few seconds as she sat and waited. Before either of us spoke, however, there was an intruder.

Derek Hogan was back. He walked quickly to my desk.

"Pardon me for a moment," he said with a silky smooth voice and a look toward Mary Lou. How he did it, I don't know—but at one and the same time, he smiled at her with a mouth expressing friendliness, while his eyes expressed utter contempt and disdain for a "weak, weepy, woman." He then gave me a momentary glance I interpreted as, "You must be weak, too, to put up with this bull."

He placed an envelope in my hand. "Just one thing I want you to do, if you can spare a minute of your time," he said smoothly with a hint of sarcasm. "Before you do anything else today, read what's in this envelope." He smiled, turned and left the room.

Mary Lou didn't seem inclined to speak immediately, or do anything else for that matter, so I said, "Excuse me," and opened the envelope. Inside were several legal-looking pages. On top was a handwritten message on one of Hogan's personalized sticky notes. It read:

> You've passed every test so far. One more
> home run, and you're on your way to
> <u>really</u> big things!
> If you can close the deal this afternoon,
> sign these papers and claim your reward.
> —*DH*

My eyes popped as I saw on page one of the documents what he was talking about. I was being offered a half-partnership in the software division! My take-home pay would double overnight as a result of this one deal alone, not to mention what we'd do the rest of the year! Looking back at the first page, I saw that it was officially dated as of last Friday. All that was required to make it a reality was to close the deal and add my own signature.

Mary Lou waited in silence as I stared into space. This was really too much! I steamrolled right over the small voice musing quietly, *I wonder why everybody is suddenly so interested in your signature?* All I could see in my mind was myself climbing a mountain of riches and glory. Hogan, Jeter, White & Mathewson: Why not? I've been working for this kind of opportunity for years … lots of long hours and painstaking work … building a reputation in this city.

Yes, what about that reputation? came a question, but it was too little too late. It's right here, literally in my grasp, if I can just push this thing through! I glanced at Mary Lou, still waiting quietly. There's no way, I thought, that you are going to get in my way. You're not going to foul this up for me.

"Mary Lou, your work hasn't been up to par lately."
Pause. She looked at me with big, steady eyes. "You're not
putting in the kind of hours and effort we expect around
here. It's even harder to understand, when someone has as
good a track record as you have."

Still, she said nothing. I decided to go another
direction.

"Mary Lou, we have always … at least, I always
thought we had … a good working relationship. You've
been extremely valuable to me in the past." Emphasis on,
"in the past." Pause. I clenched my jaw, suppressing my
anger. "Today, as you know, we are making a presentation
on an important deal. I've had to work extremely hard to
make up for the lack of help I've gotten from you." Still,
more silence. Deep breath. "So," I continued, "I need you
to make up your mind whether or not you're going to be a
member of the team. I understand personal problems, but
this is important!"

She was finally ready to speak, which she did in a low,
expressionless manner. "Dan, I used to think so, too. Even
after I got married, I was always very committed to my career. But now I'm a mother. Ever since Michael got sick,
everything's changed. I've tried to do a good job … I've really tried hard …" She couldn't contain her emotions any
longer. She began to sob softly.

I looked out the window, disgusted. This is just what I
need! I inwardly fumed.

After a minute, Mary Lou regained her composure. "I
don't know what else to say. I can't do more than I can do.
I have a husband I haven't talked to in weeks … the stress
and fatigue is killing us. I don't sleep, I don't eat. How can
I care whether or not Wiederman buys some software?"

That did it. Whatever compassion might have been there to be accessed was blown away. I just shook my head in a disgusted manner, and said, "Okay, Mary Lou. I've got nothing more to say. Do what you have to do ... go home ... go back to work ... whatever."

After a moment, she rose and walked toward the door. She stopped and turned. "You know, Dan, what really hurts? I didn't expect any understanding from the rest of them. They're all sharks. But I did expect it from you." And she was gone.

I sat, motionless for a moment, in a confusion of anger and guilt. Then I slammed my fist on my desk. No! You're not going to put this on me! I'm not responsible for everyone's life! I've got my own life to live, and I'm going for it!

I found that I was unable to regain my concentration, as my mind continued to swirl. I checked my watch: 11:15. I know. I'll go out and get a light lunch all by myself. A change of setting, getting out of this office ... I'll be all right. I headed for the elevator. I normally would have grabbed a quick sandwich at one of the shops in the building, but I felt a strong urge to get away. I needed to get in my car and drive.

I moved through the first floor lobby quickly, not wanting to engage Joe Thesecurityguard. As it turned out, he was already happily engaged in a conversation with a young businesswoman. I caught a few words: "...the Lord Jesus said, 'But seek ye first the kingdom of God, and his righteousness; and all these things...'" And I was out the door.

Quickly getting my car and exiting the garage, I headed toward the north freeway. Just three exits north of downtown and a block and a half to the right, there was a small deli called Franky's that I used to frequent when working with my previous company. It was always a nice place for a break from work, and I was already looking forward to it.

Traffic was moving at top speed. As I cruised up the freeway, I was anticipating one of Franky's great turkey sandwiches, and wondering which of his wonderful soups I should order.

Something suddenly felt odd. The road wasn't moving. Or, rather, I wasn't moving, though there had been no noticeable change or impact. All motion had completely stopped. I looked at the speedometer. It said I was going sixty-eight miles per hour, but I was not moving.

Looking to my right, I saw a middle-aged woman in a shiny red Cadillac. She stared straight ahead, stiff as a statue. So did the teenage boy in the old Chevy in front of her. He was frozen in mid-motion, flicking the ashes from his cigarette out the window.

I looked to my left. There in a green minivan was a man about my age. He was looking around with bewilderment, probably appearing much like myself. Our eyes met, registering incomprehension. Directly in front of me was a battered pick-up. Two motionless men shared the cab, while four men rode in the back with a pile of construction equipment. Three of the four were statues, while the fourth, a Hispanic young man, looked this way and that, appearing quite frightened. He eventually noticed me and shouted, gesturing wildly. I don't know Spanish, but I knew what he meant: "What is going on?!"

CHAPTER 4

꒳

I sat still in the car for a full minute, not knowing what to do. I was afraid to take my hands off the steering wheel for fear that everything would suddenly start moving again. Looking to my left, I saw that my friend in the minivan seemed as bewildered as I. He didn't know what to do, either.

The young man in the pickup was quite active, however. He leapt from side to side of the truck bed in his agitation. He tried yelling in the faces of his three co-workers, without effect. He tried shoving one of them to get a reaction, but he might as well have been trying to push a literal stone statue. The others seemed unresponsive, unmoved and unmovable.

I rolled down my window and craned my neck, looking forward and behind on the freeway. (Only afterward did it occur to me that opening my window—or moving any other object—might not be possible; but, as it turned out, it did respond). As far as the eye could see in both directions were vehicles. None were moving. Looking far to the left horizon, I could see a commercial jet that had just taken off from the airport. Closer and a little higher in the sky was a local radio station's helicopter. Both were frozen in mid-air. Even the still blades of the chopper were visible. Over a car dealership, a large American flag stretched out in the wind—except there was no wind, and the flag was without movement.

My attention was drawn again to the young Hispanic man in the pickup. After a quick look in front and behind, he hopped over the side of the truck bed, and sprinted off the freeway to the right. His thought was immediately clear. Should this weird situation end as abruptly as it started, it may be better to be out of the way. Taking a deep breath and a quick look of my own, I jumped out of my car and followed him.

We did not attempt to communicate. We just stood side by side for a couple of minutes, surveying the situation. Soon, others began to follow our lead. The man in the minivan joined us, then an older couple. A young mother trotted over as best she could, encumbered by the baby carrier she held and diaper bag over her shoulder.

Looking up and down the freeway, I could see other little groups forming like ours. Two there. Five or six there. A small clump of people near the overpass. Everyone looking around, with little conversation. What conversation there was took the form of, "What *is* this?" "What's going on?" or "It's like the *Twilight Zone* or something." All while many more people sat as frozen statues in stationary vehicles.

My ears began to attend to a sound (making me notice for the first time that, until now, there had been no sound whatsoever other than those made by ourselves: car doors, footfalls, and voices). It began as if from a distance, then moved closer and louder. It was a horn.

It was not a mechanical horn, like that of a car or train, but a musical horn. As I focused to listen, it seemed to me a natural sound. Not, in other words, a brassy horn as in modern orchestras, but the earthy, organic sound of a true animal horn. It grew louder, more powerful and insistent each moment, but it was not just a blast. It was playing notes, but not exactly a tune. As I searched for a category, the word fanfare seemed appropriate. It seemed to come from everywhere at once, rather than from a specific location.

More vivid than any observation, however, were the emotions it evoked in me. It seemed to strike at my very heart with a pain I never wanted to end. It seemed a sound from another world; another world that was, in fact, home.

The horn affected all of us the same. All conversation and movement stopped as we were transfixed by the sound. It continued to grow in volume.

It may seem that a long time must have passed since my freeway drive was interrupted, but all these actions and observations took less than ten minutes.

The horn paused, and there was a terrible explosion of thunder, thunder as I had never heard before. The earth vibrated, causing us nearly to lose our footing. I wondered for a moment: How can thunder come from a blue, cloudless sky? But almost as quickly, I realized that it was not thunder at all. It was a voice.

I perceived immediately why I had first mistaken it for thunder. Besides its sheer power, it was clearly

non-human. I don't mean it was artificial, like computer-
generated speech. It was surely the voice of an intelligent,
living being. But it was just as surely not of a *human* being.
There were none of the tones that characterize the sounds
of biological creatures.

The voice cried with the authority and power of a herald:

> Awake! Awake! Awake, sleepers, and rise
> from the dead. And the Lord, the Christ,
> shall shine upon you! Your wait has ended,
> and the day of promise has come!

> You saints who walk on the earth: Rejoice!
> Rejoice and be glad, for the day has come!
> The Lord, your Bridegroom, has pro-
> claimed this your wedding day! He calls
> you to come and meet him!

We stood speechless with hearts pounding at the herald's message. The light of what had been bright midday
sunshine began to change. As well as I can describe it, it became a rich golden tone. Something in the light itself
promised life and health, and I drew in a slow, deep breath.
It felt as wonderful as it was beautiful. The golden light almost had a taste.

"Look!" someone cried, pointing up. There, where the
noontime sun should have been was an even brighter light,
which seemed to be the source of the golden hue. The light
source was squared at four corners, and it was growing
larger. The intensity of its light was five, ten, a hundred
times brighter than the brightest sun. This I was sure of,
and yet I looked directly at it without harm. It was hard to
get a perspective to determine how far away it was. I

couldn't tell if it was as far as the blue sky, as near as the clouds, or somewhere in between. It was in the midst of these questions that I noticed for the first time: I was flying hundreds of feet above the earth.

It struck me as strange, as of any new experience, but not alarming. Having occasion to look down, I saw that my clothes had changed. I was no longer wearing a standard business suit ... what I was wearing is difficult to describe. Something like a robe or tunic, but not exactly either. Those are just the closest worldly equivalents I can use. The odd thing is that it seemed somehow more than a dead, external garment. It wasn't me, either, but something in between. Somehow part of me. No, better, somehow an extension of me.

More important than the change in my clothing, however, was the fact that I had changed. As you would expect, I noticed my hands first. They were my hands, but light and life seemed to emanate from within. Not so crudely as a human light bulb (as I had often imagined glory to appear); more as an essential property of life lived on a new frequency or plane. I intuitively knew that my body was no longer flesh and blood, but something new, immeasurably stronger and pulsating with Life of a higher order.

Looking to the side, I noticed another person who returned my gaze. Had I ever seen such a being before— one of such beauty, nobility, and glory—I would have been tempted to believe I had seen an incarnation of a Greek god. He seemed to look at me with the same astonishment.

Returning my attention to the light above, I saw that the rectangular light now filled a third of the sky. I struggled for a category. It was a hole in the heavens ... a parted curtain. No, it was obvious: It was a door.

Then, moving toward us within the door, as if striding down a walkway ... I saw *Him*.

My heart broke. It broke with joy. It broke with humiliation. Exhilaration, freedom, fear, realization ... all swirled together in a glorious mix.

The One who walked to meet us wore the lines and form of a man. He was one of us. And he was one of a kind.

He spoke. His voice carried the same power as the voice that thundered, and more. But this time it was clearly a human voice that spoke:

> Come, my beloved ones! The time has
> come! My Father has ordained this day as
> an end and as a beginning. Come and see
> the place I have prepared for you.

In the periphery of my vision I could see through the door a whole amazing ... world? ... universe? But it was impossible to take my eyes off him. The Bridegroom had come to claim his bride.

CHAPTER 5

As my feet touched down, I turned to look behind. Uncounted millions like myself, a moving galaxy of stars, streamed through the door. A great roar of joy grew in volume as more arrived, and we fell into procession behind the Lord, forming a massive river of redeemed humanity. Once more looking back, I could see the blue rectangle of earth's sky decreasing in size. The door was closing.

It was part family reunion, part victory parade. The closest earthly equivalents I can imagine are the great ticker-tape parades in New York I had seen in old newsreels that celebrated the end of World War II. I remembered a line from a Christmas carol I'd sung each season without much thought: "join the triumph of the skies." In a Bible study years ago I learned that a triumph in ancient Rome was a great parade granted to conquering generals after extraordinary victories, the only time they were permitted to bring their armies into the city. The apostle Paul

had used the triumph as an illustration of Christ's victory.
Here I was participating in its fulfillment.

I don't know how long we walked, of either time or
distance, and I know I didn't care. I could have walked for
years with this clan, my family. None of those I saw near
me were people I knew from my earthly life, but we knew
that we were one in the family of God. We walked until we
came to the crest of a huge, bowl-like landscape, and began
to descend. The Lord took his place in the center, as his
Church gathered around him. I stood at a distance that on
earth would be too far to see more than a speck of a person.
And yet, when I focused my eyes on the Lord, I found I
could see him as if he were only twenty or thirty feet away.
I would normally have paused to note this strange new experience of having telescopic vision, but I was too alarmed
to think at all. The Lord was too glorious and holy for me
to approach him so closely, even with my eyes. I backed off
to a safer visual distance of about a hundred yards away.

We all did together what we had been yearning to do,
the only thing right to do: We worshipped. We fell to our
knees and bowed our faces to the ground. We remained in
utter and complete silence for a long time—long at least by
earth reckoning—and it was the holiest experience of my
life. The silence seemed to express perfectly the honor we
wished to pay our Savior and Lord. Because all my focus
was on him, I didn't notice this at the time, but did upon
later reflection: My body was in full cooperation with my
heart for the first time in my existence. There were no wan-
dering thoughts or lapses of concentration, no weakness or
weariness of body that needed to shift position or stretch.
Apparently, my new body was a perfect servant to my liberated heart.

Eventually, we began saying together, "Holy, holy, holy is the Lord God Almighty, who was, and is, and is to come." I felt that I had never worshipped before. Yes, I had sung songs, I had prayed prayers. I had even sincerely at times wished to submit myself completely to Christ. But my spiritual best on earth always included secret reservations, holding back things and desires from the rule of God. Even when my heart was as sincere as it could be, there were clouded vision and limitations of understanding. Now, I was free to love the Lord with all my soul and give him his due: Everything. The only thought I had of myself was: This is the truest and best thing I have ever done. This is what I was made for.

We gave full honor and thanks to the Triune God: Father, Son, and Holy Spirit. The unity and spontaneity of our worship was remarkable. Without external direction, we began to sing a song together so naturally that I felt I had known it all my life:

> You are worthy to receive all honor and
> worship; for you were slain, and with your
> blood you purchased men for God from
> every tribe and tongue and people and na-
> tion. You have made them to be a king-
> dom and priests to our God, and they will
> reign upon the earth.

With one accord we made a common confession of praise:

> Worthy is the Lamb that was slain to re-
> ceive power and riches and wisdom and
> strength and honor and glory and blessing.

Then in one voice—if voice can convey the thought of the tongues of untold millions of redeemed humans, of invisible watchers and participants, and even of the elements themselves—we said,

> To him who sits on the throne, and to the
> Lamb, be blessing and honor and glory
> and dominion forever and ever.

Whether this worship lasted for hours or for years I cannot say. Time seemed of no importance.

The Lord Jesus motioned as if to speak, and all fell silent. "Welcome brethren and friends," he said. "Your place is prepared. Enter joyfully into the fullness of life. We will soon begin the great campaign to bring the kingdom of my Father to the earth. There remain many things to do before that time is at hand. I have gifts to give and honors to distribute. For the time being, I release you to rejoice, to greet one another, and to give thanks. When you hear the summons, gather to me at the Bema."

The assembly having been dismissed, a joyful roar broke out again as the redeemed of twenty centuries welcomed one another. I exchanged innumerable embraces of joy and welcome with other saints, celebrating our liberation to eternal life. It was to discover what love was for. What a milktoast experience love was on earth, I thought. At best, it was a faint shadow of this. How far short I always fell, even in my best moments. I often heard preachers' platitudes about love, such as: "Only two things on earth will last forever—God's Word and people. Loving people is an investment that will bring eternal dividends." Yeah, sure, I had yawned. Now I knew the platitude to be an understatement. And I knew that, almost without fail, I had invested unwisely, because I had invested mainly in myself.

After a while, I began to drift from the masses of people, wanting a chance to reflect. Also, for the first time, I began to pay attention to my surroundings. The beauty of this place was beyond description. How poor my conception of Heaven had always been! I realized now that whenever I tried to imagine Heaven before, I had always visualized it as *less* than earth. I thought of a place *without* form (like clouds or fog, for example), or *without* color. I saw that I had it exactly reversed. It was the earth that now appeared bland and formless. Where I was now was the birthplace or source of form and color. Form and color on earth are only two-dimensional copies of this, the real thing.

It looked like earth in some ways. It was three dimensional, but—I am straining for words—everything had more to it than the corresponding article in nature. There was vegetation of a sort, things of incredible beauty corresponding to grass and trees. What made them different? I can only answer by analogy. On earth there are inanimate objects like rocks and stones, and soulless life like trees. Both are non-conscious, yet there is a difference between the categories. Trees, while not conscious life, are certainly alive, while rocks are not. There is a qualitative difference in where they stand in the created order.

Here in the heavenlies, the very rocks and soil stand more in relation to vegetable life on earth: not conscious,

but alive in some sense. The rocks had actually cried out
along with our human voices in praise of Christ as we worshipped. They are in some way responsive servants to the
purposes of God. The trees and grass are on a higher plane:
still not conscious life, but above non-conscious life. Perhaps there is a need for an in-between category such as sub-
conscious vegetable life. If this seems far out or
incomprehensible, don't be concerned. I can do no better
explaining these observations with only earth-language as a
medium.

Colors had the same additional level of reality over
earth, but they, too, are impossible to describe. I saw for
the first time why the biblical writers who described visions of Heaven did so in such strange images: a great sea
like glass, gates of pearl, streets of gold like clear glass, wall
foundations of precious stones, and the like. Though I
hadn't seen them for myself yet, I felt I understood a little
better the weird descriptions of certain angelic beings: flying cows with eagles' wings covered with eyes, for example.
All these are feeble attempts to explain with limited earthly
language what does not fit into earthly categories or experiences. Without being able to transport you there, it would
be like asking you to imagine a fourth primary color. Your
mind is incapable of doing it. As far as my desire to describe the heavenly colors for you, the best I can do is to
suggest the impact you would feel if a color had not only a
visual quality, but also a sound or smell. Heaven is in all
ways more, not less, than earth.

Walking among the trees was a wonderful experience.
On earth there had been those almost magical moments of
natural life, when I seemed to receive a breath of paradise.
A cool morning on a camping trip while kindling the

breakfast fire. Or sitting in a rowboat fishing in the morning, watching the beginning of a glorious sunrise. In moments like those—feeling the goose-pimples on my arms, enjoying the refreshment of peace and quiet and a break from fighting and striving after things—I had often sensed a deep happiness and at the same time an aching longing for something I couldn't specify. It was a feeling I knew from childhood, in fact. I can remember wonderful summer days when I climbed trees in the woods and sat alone and quiet for hours. Just thinking and feeling. In truth, I was often praying to the God I did not yet know, and yet knew was there. Remembering those experiences, I thought: I was closer to Reality back then as a child than I was later when I grew up. I felt a sadness as I reflected on the foolish turns my life took later.

It was impossible for sadness to linger long in the heavenlies, however. The air had that same golden hue that had streamed through the door to earth, and its physical effects were even greater here. The very air rejuvenated and energized my body, as if I were being fed on every breath. Looking up, the branch of the tree under which I had paused was filled with a fruit I had never seen before. If the air itself was nutritious, what must the fruit be like? While I would dearly have loved to try a bite, something in my heart told me, "Not now." It was for a later time. Without hesitation, I obeyed the inner voice, and walked on.

I found it quite enjoyable to stroll and observe groups of people talking and laughing. Having leisure for the first time to make observations, I began to notice distinctions between the people. We were all alike … and yet not identical. We all bore the likeness of our Lord, and yet there were some differences beyond personalities. Paying closer attention, it seemed that people fell into categories of similarity. They weren't quite races, as we would call them on earth, but people fell into groupings. It surprised me for a moment. Racial distinctions had been the cause of so much suffering and so many wars and atrocities on earth that I had assumed that God would eliminate the problem by eliminating distinctions. A moment of reflection later, though, and I understood: God likes variety. Distinctions are a good thing. It is only sin that has taken the good thing God created and caused it to go bad. God's desire is to show unity—perfect oneness—in diversity. If the same pattern held true in this subject that I had observed in other things, the heavenly distinctions behind races on earth would prove to be more precise and varied, and the unity among them would prove to be more powerful than I ever imagined. As the many facets of a diamond multiply the beauty and glory of the gem, God reveals his glory through a many-faceted creation.

While I was sitting on a couch-sized rock thinking these things through, I became aware of a presence. I heard no one. I saw no one. But I felt I was not alone.

Then I heard a voice: "Daniel Mathewson. I wish to speak with you, Sir, if I may be permitted."

I stood up and looked around me. Even in the act of doing so, something inside told me I would see nothing. The words had been spoken by a non-human voice, like the herald that had announced the Lord's coming, though at an appropriately lower volume. It had that same artificial, but not mechanical, quality.

I was being addressed by an angel.

CHAPTER 6

❧

I was not afraid, but I was unnerved. Not only was I being spoken to by an invisible being, but by one I assumed to have lived for millennia—an immortal spirit. I felt tiny and weak, somewhat like a small child called to the principal's office. I stood speechless, baffled as to the proper way to respond. It finally dawned on me that the spirit had asked my permission to speak. I stammered, "Of course … please…"

"It is my honor to greet you, and be able to speak to you at last," said the voice.

The voice seemed to emanate from a point a few feet away, about five feet above the ground. Having a fixed location did not help my comfort level, though. I didn't know what to do, what to say, what the proper protocol might be. Should I bow? Salute? Should I speak to that mid-air spot which seemed to be the location of the voice?

My confusion must have been evident. "For many of your people," the voice said, "it seems easier if we assume a similar form to yourself. Shall I?"

I didn't know what to say. I made some inane reply like, "Well … whatever you wish."

There was a blinding flash, and a being appeared before me glowing like a sun; a sun with a human shape. Startled, I instinctively recoiled, throwing a hand up before my eyes.

As if someone had turned down a dimmer switch, the light quickly diminished, until the being only moderately glowed. "Are you hurt?" he asked. When I assured him I was all right, he said, "Please pardon me, Sir. Is this intensity more suitable for your senses?"

"Yes, this is fine," I replied. I would have been instantly incinerated to ashes had I faced such a being at close quarters in my earthly body. "I was not hurt, just surprised." I did not know what to say or do, so I waited silently. In the presence of one so obviously superior, there was nothing to do but submit and obey. Was I to be given orders?

"Daniel Mathewson," he began, "since the day you were born, I have watched over you and served you, though I have been forbidden to reveal myself to you. Today I have discharged my stewardship, and I await your command."

I was completely at a loss. Stewardship? He awaits *my* command? Then, a glimmer of light. "Do you mean you are my guardian angel?" I asked.

"The answer is yes, though 'guardian angel' is not what we would call ourselves. I have indeed served you and protected you on many occasions."

"And ..." (I only fearfully completed this question) "did you say ... are you saying ... that you are here to serve *me*?"

"Yes. Though we are the eldest of God's creatures and are gifted with powers and knowledge vastly beyond yours, it is our greatest honor and pleasure to offer humble service to the heirs of salvation."

I continued to be dumbfounded. How could a creature so much greater in intellect and power (and in who-knows-what other ways?) be in a servant position to one like me? Here is a spirit who has outlived continents, with power that humans would measure on a nuclear scale. Here am I, a member of a race part spiritual and part animal, with intellect and physical strength an infinitesimal fraction of his. Beyond this, I am a member of a fallen race. A creature who has sampled evil and sin, and enjoyed the taste. I am morally farther below this being than an amoeba is below a man.

I wasn't even sure if I had the strength to continue standing in his presence. I felt a strong urge to fall at his feet in humiliation, but an inner voice told me that to do so would be wrong. As a compromise, I half-fell, half-sat down again on the rock.

The angel continued to stand before me, almost like a soldier at attention. What does one say to an angel? Finally I asked, motioning to my side, "Would you like to sit?"

"As you wish," he answered. Watching him sit down beside me, I found his movements interesting. They were almost natural, almost human. Of course, the "almost" means they were not natural or human. I found myself speculating on what made the difference. I decided that the angel's movements were too perfect, too smooth, similar to a foreigner who has become fluent in English. It is the foreigner's perfect English grammar that gives him away. A native-born English speaker uses slang and what is actually poor grammar in a natural way, and communicates clearly. A human's movement is similar. He moves in a natural, often individually quirky way. The angel had learned to move a human-like body in a humanlike manner through observation, but his actions were artificial—too smooth and perfect.

Feeling more comfortable in his presence, I began to look at him more closely. His body seemed to be made of pure light. But it was (if this makes any sense) solid light. The color is difficult to describe, because it was constantly in motion and changing. It seemed pure silver, then slightly golden, then more on the orange side with a flash of red. The surface of his "skin" was perfectly smooth. My guess is that it was also very thin—egg-shell thin. I had no doubt, however, that it was also more solid and dense than the strongest metal alloy on earth. Overall, I had the impression that the angel's body was hollow inside (as we would describe it), somewhat like the Invisible Man wearing a masquerade costume. It was merely an appearance he assumed temporarily for the convenience and comfort of lesser creatures like myself. He expressed no emotions I could perceive. He made no facial expressions and used no gestures when speaking. In that way, it was almost like talking to a department store mannequin.

My first impression was that he wore no clothing, but as I became used to his appearance, it seemed as if he were wearing a very slight, translucent garment. Some kind of tunic or robe that fell and moved like linen. I'm inclined to think that his garment was not strictly necessary (as on earth, for modesty), but was rather an expression of dignity. Possibly a sign of office or rank.

After these observations (which actually took less time to make than they do to describe), I decided to try conversation. "So," I began, "what shall I call you? Do you have a name?" I immediately flinched, feeling I had asked a stupid question.

The angel still showed no emotion. "Yes. In your speech my name means 'Flame of God.' The kinsmen of our Lord would have pronounced it 'Uriel.' You will undoubtedly meet others of my kind called Uriel, as well. In our own speech, there are many types and nuances to 'flame,' and so each has his own unique name. However, to explain the distinctions in your language would take many words, and so each of us will seem to have the same name until you have learned enough of our language to understand the difference."

Flame of God seemed an appropriate name for the spirit. The shifting colors I had observed in his appearance did look like fire. "Uriel," I said, "I have so many questions I would like to ask that I hardly know where to begin. Would you tell me about yourself?"

"That would take a long time," he replied, as a pinkish glow flickered. "I watched as our Lord made your world. I fought in the Great War and saw the Enemy and his legions defeated. I have served with mighty commanders, even under Michael, whose name perhaps you know."

I had no trouble imagining Uriel as terrible in war (that is, "terrible" in the classic sense: "inspiring terror and dread"). As he spoke of the Great War, his colors had shifted from orange to yellow to purest silver—silver like the brightest star in the heavens. What would he be like in battle if he unleashed the awesome power he was so obviously veiling?

"Yes, I have heard of Michael," I answered. "The Bible calls him an archangel. Am I right that an archangel is a chief or general?"

"That is correct. In the created order, only the Fallen One was greater. To serve at the command of Michael is a rare and great honor."

"And what of yourself?" I asked. "Are you a leader or an officer?" I felt such awe at the power of Uriel that it seemed a natural question.

"No, Daniel Mathewson," he replied, his color shifting to that rosy pink again. "I am not great. I am of the lowest rank of my order. I would be known as a foot soldier in your world."

Thinking of Uriel as an ordinary private in the celestial military only multiplied my awe. "And you have watched over me?" I asked. "You spoke of serving and protecting me."

"Yes. All service to God is a great pleasure. And yet there is one service for which all of us especially long: the honor of being appointed as steward—or guardian as you say—of a child of God. I was privileged to witness or serve at many of the events of which you have read in your Bible and in your history books. However, this one great desire of my heart was still unfulfilled."

The angel paused. His colors turned a rich golden hue. Neither his body nor expression betrayed any emotions, but I had the distinct impression that he was deep in thought.

He continued: "Centuries in your world had passed, and then we could see gathering signs indicating that the

Lord's time was close at hand. Had I never been selected for this service, I would have bowed to God's will and rejoiced in the blessings bestowed upon others. But I continued to hope, while hope was still possible."

A pink flame flashed across him, and he turned almost red. "Then, the day! God's word commissioned me, and I flew to earth with joy I cannot express. You, Daniel Mathewson, were soon to be born, and I was granted stewardship over you. I have protected you from natural dangers, from illnesses, from attacks of the Enemy's agents, even from your own foolishness. I have encouraged you, strengthened you, and comforted you. Finally, my commission was to bring you safely to the heavenlies. That is why I said that I have discharged my stewardship."

My head reeled from overload, but worse was the shame I felt. His reference to my "foolishness" was too kind. What could a holy creature feel toward me after watching me all my life? After all the ugly behavior toward others ... all the evident selfishness ... all that had gone on in private (now realizing there is no such place)?

"*All* my life you have been with me?" I asked softly, hanging my head. I wanted to disappear. I wanted him to go away. His knowledge was too great and intimate.

"Do not grieve, Daniel Mathewson," he said. "I have seen the burden sin has placed on the shoulders of the children of Adam. I have observed the harm and the destruction and grief that resulted from sin. But remember this: I saw evil and sin in its purest and most awful form. I knew the Fallen One before he fell, and I observed what sin can do to pervert the most powerful creature of God, as well as the many others he seduced into following him. That was only the beginning of the terrible history of evil. Your first father and mother believed the lie the Enemy whispered to them, and all members of your race have since been born devoid of spiritual life and possessing the inner infection. You are born believing the lie: that a being created by God can rebel against its Creator, can step out of its dependent, obedient relationship with him, and can attain godlike status—can in effect become God's equal and apart from him find life.

"You are born rebels, born into a rebellion of greater proportions than you know. It forces you either to view God as your great enemy and fear, or to remake him in your own imagination into something else—into another god you do not need to fear. All your lives you are driven by sin and selfishness, while a vacuum in your heart hungers for meaning and significance, for love and acceptance, for a sense of identity—desires that can be completely satisfied only through union with the same God from whom you are trying to flee. The history of your world, with all its injustice and destruction and pain, is a testimony to the results of believing the lie.

"That is why the day you became a child of God, being reconciled to him through faith in the Lord Jesus Christ, was the day of my greatest joy—greater even than the day I received my stewardship. Many others in the heavenlies joined me in rejoicing over you. We watch in amazement and give praise to God who has worked such a wonder, defeating evil and making a way to adopt sinners into his family and remake them in the image of his Son.

"I have indeed watched you writhe under sin's influence, and watched you fall many times. I have grieved for you. As I watched you struggle with temptations, as I listened to the seduction of the Enemy's lies, as I observed the hurt you inflicted on others and the hurt others inflicted on you, I grew to understand and hate evil all the more. Praise be to God that, in his time, he will destroy sin and evil forever!"

Once again as he was speaking, the angel's flaming colors shifted from orange to yellow to purest, brightest silver. It finally dawned on me that this might be the way an angel's emotions can be perceived. Not as with humans through bodily gestures, expressions, and voice, but by color. There had been some consistency: Silver seemed to indicate his war-like disposition, hatred of evil, and zeal for justice; gold his pensive, meditative mood; pink seemed to show pleasure, or even some angelic equivalent of shyness or humor; red was joy. I knew better than to suppose that these observations were more than compass directions, but I felt I was on the right track, nonetheless. I determined to watch for more indications.

Uriel continued. "Throughout your life, I longed for this day, the day your salvation from sin would be consummated, and your struggle would be over." Rosy-toned flames with flashes of red burned across his humanlike form. Then he said, "Daniel Mathewson, I have been waiting and hoping for this day for another reason. I would like to make one request, to ask you to grant me a favor."

What "favor" could an angel want to ask of *me*?

Chapter 7

❧

Once again, I was baffled and speechless. What "favor" could I possibly offer an ageless, powerful spirit who has lived in the heavenlies since the creation of all things, serving at the direct command of God?

"Uriel," I began haltingly, "you have looked after me and served me in ways I am only beginning to understand. I owe you more than I even know. What can I offer you?"

"My desire, Sir," answered the angel, "is to be permitted to continue as your servant." My questioning look must have been obvious, because he went on. "My stewardship was discharged, as I have said, on the day I delivered you here. Should you no longer desire my presence or service, I will return and await God's bidding. However, he has granted to his children this authority: to command or release from service those who have been their unseen companions. I wish, if you find this pleasing, to remain with you."

"But why, Uriel?" I asked. "With all you are capable of doing, why do you want to remain with me?"

"Because it is a joy, first," he answered. "But perhaps even more, because I wish to learn from you."

"*Learn* from me? What could you learn from *me*?" I stood up, gesturing in surprise with extended arms and upright palms. Uriel, in the manner of a servant, immediately stood as well.

"Many things!" The angel flashed with silver and gold flames. "Long we have watched in joy and amazement God's mighty and unforeseen works among men. I have seen generations pass away. I have seen nations rise and fall. I have watched individual men and women fight the good fight of truth, and I have watched men and women fight against the things of God. I have observed children of Adam practice the secret things of darkness, and I have watched great saints contend for their Lord and his people in battles they scarcely comprehended. I have become familiar with many works of God and all of human experience that can be observed. But I, and all of my kind, remain outsiders. We are only observers of the relationship God has made between himself and men.

"I want to learn what it means to receive grace. What is it like to be forgiven? What is it like to rejoice in a salvation freely received, yet purchased at a great cost: the blood of the Lamb of God?

"What is it like to be made in God's image? And now, having been redeemed, what is it like to share the nature and image of our Lord, the Son of the living God? What is it like to possess the indwelling presence of the Holy Spirit?

"You humans are spiritual beings, as we are, and yet you are housed in a body. What is it like to feel? We know pleasure, as you do, but it is of our minds and souls. How is it different to taste, and smell, and feel? What is it like to eat a fruit created for you by our Lord? What is it like to be a child, then to grow older? What is it like to have a mother and father?

"I want to understand music. We worship God with all our souls, and before this time, much more purely than any child of Adam has ever done. And yet, God has given you the gift of song. I can observe your actions and reactions, but I cannot understand how it comes from your hearts or what it means. How does it feel to sing?

"I want to understand love. The pure love that comes from God we know, and that love we share among ourselves. But God has created something new and more in men. What is love like between a husband and wife? What is it like to become one with another, to be united in soul and life? What is it like to produce children, who are extensions of your lives, and yet distinct individuals?

"What is it like to laugh, and what does it mean? Of all human actions, it is to me the most mysterious."

I threw up my hands. "All right! Enough!" I laughed. "Uriel, I'm not sure I know how to answer your questions. It may be as hard for me to answer them as for you to understand them, but I'll try. I confess it is hard for me to understand why you would wish to remain in my presence any longer than you already have. But I welcome your company, and I invite you to stay with me as long as you please. I probably have just as many questions I want to ask you. It seems we'll have enough subjects to occupy us for a good long time."

Uriel's flames flashing pink and red, he replied, "Time is not an issue here."

"Why don't we walk a while?" I said, and we started across the countryside. I felt the need for a break from the furious pace of conversation we had been keeping. There were so many subjects raised, each of which could have led to an extensive conversation in itself, that I wanted to let my thoughts settle. There was going to be no lack of intellectual stimulation in the heavenlies! Uriel accompanied me in silence, allowing me to set the verbal, as well as walking, pace. Assuming that he was not subject to humanlike impatience, I felt free to do so.

The landscape seemed to be part garden, part park; open areas interspersed with intimate areas of woods. Here and there I could see other people engaged in conversation. Some, like myself, were talking with angelic beings, presumably also their stewards. More common were small groups, little clusters of people speaking in an animated and joyful manner, punctuated by laughter. Hearing the laughter, and with my attention recently drawn to it by Uriel's question, I noticed how healthy and holy it sounded. Laughter on earth covered a range from innocent happiness and humility to indecent jokes and cruelty. Here, laughter conveyed only the pure expression of joy, fellowship, and truth. It was as beautiful as music, as holy as worship. I heard in the laughter of the saints the humble submission of a creature who knows his true relation to his Creator, and his true proportion to other created beings; his true position as a child of God by grace; and his joyful and willing acceptance of the last place, truly allowing the Host to elevate him to the place of honor at the proper time. Laughter here was a beautiful song of freedom.

My thoughts drifted back to where we had ended our conversation. "Uriel, you mentioned that time is not an issue here. I would like to know more. For example, when the Lord came for us, time had stopped on earth. Is that what you mean? Can time stop again if we want it to?"

Uriel's golden-orange form turned to rose-pink again. He had said that angels don't understand laughter, but I had the distinct impression this angel frequently found me amusing. "That is not the right way to say it, Daniel Mathewson. Time did not stop. What you observed and experienced was eternity breaking in. Time is not absolute. Your impression that it is comes from your earth-bound experience. Your race has only observed time moving in one direction at a constant rate. It has been created by God in the same way as what you call the laws of nature, as constants within which and against which you may live lives where real action and choices are possible. But these things are not absolutes to their Creator. To our God, all things are his servants and act according to his will. In the heavenlies, time is both broader and deeper.

"Time did not stop on earth at all. It was pierced by eternity. To those left behind, there was no experience of time stopping, or lapse of time at all. To them, it all happened in the twinkling of an eye. Their experience has been an instantaneous disappearance of many others, followed by logical and predictable consequences. Time continued on earth, according to their perceptions, and many significant events have occurred even as we have spoken together."

It took me a few moments to turn my assumptions inside-out, but Uriel's explanation began to make sense as I reflected on my experience and observations on the

freeway: the frozen people, including those whom the Hispanic young man could not budge despite exerting all his
strength; the helicopter with its still blades visible, and the
jet plane hanging in midair; the flag extended motionless,
despite the lack of wind; the absence of sounds. They all
made sense when viewed as a single instant of time, like a
solitary movie frame. Of course there could be no movement or sound! "I think I'm beginning to understand," I
said, "but I still don't see how time could be deeper."

"You will see more," Uriel replied. "To our Lord, time
can be as constant or elastic as needed to accomplish his
purpose. This will be evident to you at the Bema."

"Yes, and what exactly is the Bema? The Lord said we
would be summoned there. It sounds like a holy and solemn thing, but I don't know what it is."

"The Bema is the Judgment Seat," Uriel answered. "It
would have been called a *tribunal* during some periods of
your history. It is the great seat from which our Lord will
judge his people. He will call for an account of your stewardship, and he will dispense honors and rewards."

I can only describe my inner reaction to this news as
holy fear. Not fear as in facing an enemy, or fear of being
harmed by a malicious person. But fear in its truest sense:
the overwhelming awe that I am a creature, and a fallen
one at that, about to face my Lord, my Creator, my
Redeemer, the true and righteous Judge. The only One
who knows all the truth, who is Truth. And he will evaluate me.

Uriel seemed to understand my unspoken feelings.
"Yes. It is a fearful thing to come face to face with our
Lord. He is a righteous King who judges according to
truth. But he also acts in mercy, and in kindness, and in

grace. He is your Savior and he loves you, Daniel Mathewson."

That I knew. But, somehow, his love seemed as fearsome as his justice.

Once, when I was a child, I had a terrific abdominal pain. I lay on a couch, curled into a ball, groaning. I gritted my teeth. I held my stomach. But I would not tell my mother. Why? Because I knew what she would do. She would take me directly to the doctor, who would do terrible things to me. I feared the doctor most of all, not because he was evil, but because he was good. It was because he was good that he would do things to me that hurt, and that is exactly what he did. He put me in the hospital, cut me open, and removed my appendix. It did hurt! And I got well.

My fear of the Lord's judgment was like the dread a person in deep financial trouble might feel about talking to an accountant; or the uneasiness a person in bondage to sin and destructive behavior might feel about going to a wise pastor for biblical counsel. These are not fears of what a malicious enemy would do, but fear of the medicine (real or figurative) that the good doctor, accountant, or pastor would prescribe.

These are, however, only feeble earthly examples to try to illustrate the proper and holy reverence I felt at the prospect of the Lord's evaluation. Uriel's reference to the Judgment Seat reminded me of what I knew from my earthly Bible study. The Bema does not refer to a criminal trial where a defendant is tried for the purpose of determining guilt and punishment. That is what the unbelieving world will face at the Great White Throne judgment described in Revelation. The Bema is where a steward (or contestant, using the language of sports) is evaluated for commendation (or a prize). Punishment is not in view at all, only reward or the lack thereof.

I felt the Holy Spirit strengthening and encouraging my heart, reminding me of the wonderful truth: I was no longer flesh and blood. My sins had been erased through the blood of the Lord Jesus, and I had been credited with his righteousness by faith alone. It was as a justified, forgiven saint that I would face the Lord of all creation.

In the midst of these thoughts, as if on cue, a horn began to sound a fanfare. It blew majestically, regally, across the blue skies and golden atmosphere of the heavenlies.

"That is the summons," said Uriel.

"Let's go," I said.

CHAPTER 8

⁓

The call to the Bema had come. I felt calm and confident—not in myself, but in the Lord. I knew that whatever the Lord Jesus does is good, just, and right. He can be completely trusted, and I was completely willing to commit all judgment to him.

How different this confidence was from my natural state on earth, even though I was redeemed! There, my innate tendency as a fallen man was to distrust God. I knew deep down that I was a rebel, and I projected my hostility onto God, assuming he felt the same about me. He is, of course, hostile toward sin, and apart from Jesus Christ, his just wrath would be directed toward me. But God demonstrated his love for me by sending his Son to die for me while I was still a sinner. Through faith in Jesus Christ, I was saved from the wrath of a holy God. His perfect love was meant to release me from fear, so I could enjoy a trusting, loving relationship with him.

Even so, I began to see how much effort I had spent running from him. Even as a Christian knowing the gospel, I wasted time cowering in the shadows, whipped by my conscience. That guilt and fear caused me to miss out on much of the intimate relationship he wanted to enjoy with me. Plus, unresolved guilt caused me to run from him who was my only source of help, practically guaranteeing that I would continue the same sinful patterns. There was no reason for it, for the cross of Jesus Christ is the one sufficient remedy for genuine guilt. Again, my own stubborn heart was to blame. What joy and freedom it is, I thought, to have shed indwelling sin along with mortal flesh!

"How shall we get to the Bema?" I asked Uriel.

"I will conduct you there, if it pleases you," he answered. "I can do so in the same way I brought you to the heavenlies. However, it may be better for me to relinquish this form. May I have your permission?"

"Whatever you think best," I answered, and the figure of light disappeared. In its place was what seemed to be a cloud. Maybe "glowing smoke" is the best way to say it. The form was not solid. I could see through it at several points. Its borders rolled and waved, yet it had finite limits. Pulling back my perspective to take in the entire being, I finally recognized what I was seeing. Though it had the shifting, non-solid properties of a cloud, the form was roughly man-shaped with two great winglike projections from the "shoulders" (I am obviously again straining for categories). There was no distinguishable face. This may seem odd, but everywhere seemed to be the face. It dawned on me that perhaps visions of angels in this form were the historical basis of the persistent tradition in art that they are winged creatures. Also, being spirits without bodies, they perceive in all directions at once. Hence, the notion that their bodies are "covered with eyes."

"I could transport you without a visible form," Uriel explained, "but you may feel more comfortable traveling and conversing with one you can see. Will this form be satisfactory?" I gave my assent and we were off.

Flying above the world of the heavenlies was an experience marvelous and beyond description. Given a higher perspective, the land appeared to be made of precious gems. Every color of the heavenly rainbow was richly represented in a mosaic of heartbreaking beauty. In the sky were countless other saints converging on a point in the distance still too far to make out. Seeing them, I noticed that there were no birds in the air, and, following quickly upon that thought, I realized that I had seen no animal life at all. Perhaps the animal kingdom was uniquely prepared for man's earthly companionship, or for a different time. Another question to file away.

"Uriel," I said, "you have mentioned more than once that you brought me here. Do you mean it was you who carried me when I was flying to meet the Lord in the air?"

"Yes," he answered, "though you will not always need my help. Before long you will learn to conduct yourself wherever you wish in the Lord's service."

I reacted with surprise, and he continued. "Your new body has many properties you do not yet know. Do you not remember the accounts of our Lord after his resurrection? He appeared and disappeared, and passed through closed rooms to the surprise of his former companions. Those were only hints of his bodily changes. The same is true of yours. As you were created in the image of God to live in your earthly body, so now you are recreated in the image of our Lord, possessing a heavenly body like his."

I reflected in silence for a time, digesting this new information. Finally I said, "Uriel, there is much I find hard to understand. For one thing, you speak of having been with me all my life and protecting me. I never saw you or knew you were there. I can't recall ever being saved from danger."

"Daniel Mathewson," he replied, "you were in danger every day of your life. Because your vision is so limited, and also because of your inborn self-centeredness, you humans on earth do not realize how fragile your lives are. Besides natural physical dangers on every hand, agents of the Enemy were always looking for people to destroy. They would have been glad to kill you at any opportunity—not because you are individually so significant in the larger conflict, but simply because our Lord loved you. They are impotent to harm him, so they try instead to destroy those things he loves." Uriel paused for a moment. "Before very long," he continued, "he will take away even their freedom to do that much."

"And you also mentioned protecting me from my own foolishness," I said.

"That is true, Sir. Foolishness of all kinds. Childhood foolishness, such as playing with dangerous things. I once prevented you from being electrocuted when you were small. You were playing with a tool behind a chair in your grandparents' home, and you decided to insert it into an electric socket. You might have died, but I saved you. On another occasion when you were a toddler, you wandered out of your house into a construction area next door. You got stuck in the mud as a large machine was approaching you. I alerted the operator, who noticed you and took you home. Then, as a young adult you took foolish chances. I once saved you from drowning when you were caught in a fast-moving river in a canoe. Do you recall? Your canoe got pinned to a tree, and began to fill with water. Rather than waiting for help, you decided to get out and try to free it yourself. Your feet slipped out from under you, and you went under the water. It was my hand that pulled yours up and located a place for you to grip and then helped you find your footing.

"You were often sinfully foolish as a young man. I safely conducted you home to bed on three occasions after you drank to the point of intoxication. I once kept you from driving into a freeway overpass."

Fraternity parties! I winced at the memory, and at how idiotic I had been so many times in my life. It never occurred to me before that the preservation of my natural life to adulthood was as much a gift of God's sovereign grace as was my salvation through Jesus Christ.

"I even protected you the very day our Lord came for his Church," Uriel continued.

"How so?" I asked, remembering nothing unusual.

"While you were driving to work in the morning, I could tell you were in a foul mood. Do you recall the other car that cut you off on the freeway? There was an enemy agent influencing the driver of that vehicle, blinding him to good sense. He would have struck your car and possibly killed you had I not prevented it. Then, I could see that in your own foul temper you were about to chase after him—for what reason I could not comprehend. I maneuvered the other vehicles around you to hedge you in."

"You prevented me from hurting myself," I said, as much to myself as to Uriel.

"Yes, Sir."

"What a trial it must have been to watch over a creature like me."

"Not a trial, Sir. A joy."

We flew in silence for a time, and I enjoyed gazing at the beauty of the heavenlies. I looked to the left and noticed another saint flying fairly close to me, though without a visible companion. Looking at me, she gave me a smile so brilliant and beautiful as to nearly erase my vision of the landscape.

It occurred to me that I had consciously thought the word "she" for the first time. While I had noticed earlier the common characteristics that seemed to correspond to races, I had not thought about the sexes at all. As I looked at this saint, for whom a feminine pronoun seemed completely appropriate, I realized that none of the people I had seen showed sexual characteristics. I also noted with great joy that I felt no trace of lust, sexual attraction, or even the fleeting notice one always experienced on earth in the presence of the opposite sex.

As I recalled my observations of the saints during my time so far in the heavenlies, I decided that people did fall into categories like men and women. The sexes were indeed here, but, in fact, "sex" was not the right word. Gender, yes, but not sex.

Thinking about it further, it made sense. The Bible says that when God created the creature called man, he made *them* male *and* female. Both express aspects of God's character, and, united in marriage, a mystery which is greater than the sum of the two. Masculine and feminine express gender, being reflections or facets of God's nature, while sex is gender applied to the biological, physical level. Since there will be no marriage or reproduction in the heavenlies, sex has been shed along with the earthly body of flesh and blood. Gender, however, the principle behind sex, goes on as an expression of God's glory in redeemed men. In fact, more than goes on. Like all other things I had witnessed, gender in heaven will be richer and more glorious than it ever could be on earth.

My wife, Susan, came to mind for the first time. How odd, I thought, that only now am I thinking of my wife and loved ones.

"Uriel," I said, "I haven't yet met anyone I knew from earth. I'm sure many of them are here." I didn't know how to put into words the question in my mind.

"That is most likely, Sir, because you did not wish to see anyone," the angel answered. "For, rest assured, when you wish to see someone, you may do so."

"That seems strange to me. On earth I would have guessed that meeting my loved ones would be the first thing I'd want to do."

"I do not know the answer to that," Uriel replied. "Perhaps you first needed time to learn about life in the heavenlies. Perhaps the Lord wills that you have time to prepare for the Bema. Perhaps you have simply not been ready to meet them. I do not know. I do not believe it to be important. As you have learned, there is time to do whatever you wish to do in the heavenlies. All of your desires will be answered."

Returning my attention to our travels, I could see ahead a great circle. It seemed to be the destination of all the shining saints I saw streaming in from every direction.

As we approached, I began to feel that I was looking at something familiar. I thought to myself, I know I have seen this before, but what is it?

Getting closer, I suddenly recognized what I was seeing. It was a stadium ... or what would be called a stadium on earth. The view seemed momentarily familiar, I now realized, because on earth I had flown in planes over sports stadiums.

"Is that the Bema?" I asked.

"Yes," Uriel answered. "That is where the saints will gather for judgment."

I believe on earth I would have felt disappointed or let down to discover that the Bema would take place in something so commonplace as a stadium. But before I could even entertain such a thought, my mind answered, What else could it be? If you were to gather a great crowd of spectators to observe an event, what structure could be so logical as a large circle with sloping stands for seats?

As we descended, my reaction of commonplace was overcome by growing astonishment. From a distance it appeared to be an ordinary stadium. Now I was able to gauge its size. It was positively enormous! Earthly arenas were molehills compared to this. This was the size of a city on earth ... no, a whole metropolitan area! Tens of millions could gather here! For all I know, billions!

We touched down outside the walls in the midst of a huge gathering crowd. As before, there were happy conversations and embraces of greeting, but the sound was somehow different. It had a reverent tone of holy expectation. Joyful, but serious.

It was time for judgment to begin with the household of God.

CHAPTER 9

I stood looking up at the facade of the great arena. Its height on earth would have been measured in dozens of stories. I couldn't begin to guess its circumference. The facade seemed to be made of the same kind of stone that I observed commonly in the countryside, a grayish-white color. It was ornately carved, woven with gold leaf, and encrusted with enormous gems of all colors. All around the wall were large portals leading inside.

"Let's go in," I said, and began walking toward the nearest entrance.

"Wait, Sir," interrupted Uriel, who had resumed his man-shaped form. I stopped and turned. "I cannot accompany you in this form, or any other. The Bema is a great and solemn occasion for the royal family of our Lord. Other than those assisting in an official capacity, we servants are permitted to witness the proceedings only in our unseen presence. We are truly outsiders in this event, though we possess a keen interest in it. We earnestly desire to see the saints of God receive honor and glory for their faithful perseverance and participation in the holy conflict."

"The Lord's will is surely right, Uriel," I said, "though I would have enjoyed having you with me. There is much I will want to understand that you could explain and interpret to me."

Uriel stood silent and motionless for a minute, then he spoke. "The Lord has granted me permission to play that role for you. I must remain unseen and we may not speak aloud, but I can answer your questions during the judgment."

"How can that be?" I asked. "How can you answer my questions if we are not allowed to speak?"

"As master and servant, we are able to communicate to one another without spoken words," Uriel answered. "Did I not say that your new body has many properties you have not yet discovered? This is one. You need only apply your will to your unspoken thoughts, and I will hear you. I can reply in the same way. Indeed, I could do so to you even on earth, though only in a shadowy form. Many times I whispered thoughts to you that you heard without hearing."

Once again I was surprised. "I don't recall ever hearing anything," I said. "I never knew of your presence."

"No, not of my presence," he replied. "However, there were many occasions when our Lord directed me to prompt you or encourage you. Think back. Were there not times when you were pondering alone, discouraged, and portions of the Holy Scripture came to your mind and strengthened your resolve? Were there not times mysterious to you when a person's face or name came to mind without apparent cause, and you responded to find that there was a real need? Did you not as a parent sometimes become suddenly alert to a danger to your child?"

"Yes, I can remember times like those. And they were your doing?"

"Many times they were. Yes, Sir."

A few months before our call to the heavenlies, I had one of those experiences. I was sitting at my desk working when a person's face flashed across the vision of my mind. It was a man named Bill, a fellow member of my Sunday School class. I could identify no reason why I thought of him, but now that I had, it seemed to me that I had not seen him in a few months. We had once struck up a friendship on a weekend retreat through discovering that we dealt with similar pressures and issues at work. We never developed the friendship very far, but I liked him. Where had he been? I looked up his work number and called, only to hear: "Mr. Tucker is no longer with this company. Can someone else help you?" I then dialed his home number and found him. Yes, he had been out of work for two weeks. Though he was working hard to conceal his fear and discouragement, I could tell he was seriously struggling. We had a forty-five minute conversation about looking for employment, and I gave him a few leads. At the end he thanked me profusely, and it seemed he had been greatly encouraged. The Lord had used me to help another member of his body.

That was one of many stories that came to mind, when I had responded to the inner prompting and found that I had done something of value for someone. Sadly, I could also remember when I chose to ignore it. What good works have I passed by, preoccupied, when I missed an opportunity to be used by God?

"Come, then, Uriel," I said, "and speak to me as the Lord allows." He disappeared from view, and I entered the nearest tunnel.

The portal was understandably very long and wide, in accordance with the proportions of the arena. The many people streaming in spoke, if at all, in low whispers. Finally I came to the interior, and again I was struck breathless by its size. It seemed that I was looking miles across to the seats opposite. The rows rose up a long way toward the sky and downward to a small center. The inner construction appeared to be pure white marble, the seats actually being steps or like a marble bench, formed in a perfect circle around the inner circumference. Being built like steps, each had a back that reached up to the next layer of seats. Hundreds of millions could gather here, I thought. Millions already had, as the seats were about two-thirds filled. Turning to the left, I walked a while, then moved down a few rows and selected a seat.

What had Uriel said about communicating by my mind alone? "Apply your will," he said. I decided to try it. "Uriel," I thought, "can you hear me?" I felt silly, as if I were testing a walkie-talkie. But it worked, for in my mind's ear I heard, "Yes, Sir. This is the way we can converse without speaking. I will be present and available to serve you."

Another thing I wanted to try out was that odd ability to apply telescopic vision. "Uriel, when we first arrived, I found I was able to see the Lord up close, even though he was far away. How can I do that?"

"In the same way in which we are speaking," came the answer. "I do not have eyes as you have, but I presume you will be able to see what you wish by training your eyes on the object and applying your will."

I decided to try it. I looked directly across the stadium to a location that was several miles away by earth measurements, and willed (I cannot think of a more precise term in earth language) to see up close. Just as a camera zooms in, I found I could see the people seated there as if they were a few feet away. One looked directly at me and gave me a smile and wave of welcome. I waved back at him.

I next trained my vision on the innermost circle at the center of the arena. There was a great raised platform, with many steps leading up to it, and a throne positioned at the center: the Bema.

My attention was then drawn to the area behind the Bema. No one had chosen to sit in those sections, though for what reason I could not tell. There did not seem to be any physical barriers, but people had apparently deliberately avoided a large wedge-shaped area directly behind the Judgment Seat. Remembering the occasions in the heavenlies when I received intuitive knowledge, such as when I was directed not to eat the fruit, I decided that God must have moved his people to leave that area open.

Someone came and sat down on my left, greeting me with a smile. "Hello," I said. I hadn't yet had any substantial conversations with other people, having been occupied with observations and discussions with Uriel. I felt like getting to know someone. "My name is Daniel Mathewson," I said, extending my hand.

He shook it. "I am Gensuke," he said. "Where and when are you from?"

"I am from the United States," I replied, and hesitated. Nobody had ever asked me *when* I am from. "I was born in the last half of the twentieth century. I was alive when the Lord came for us."

"What a blessing to be walking on the earth at his coming!" my new friend exclaimed. "I am from Japan. We did not know in what time we lived according to your reckoning, but from conversations with others, it seems I lived in what you knew as the seventeenth century. It was a time when ships came from Europe to trade, also carrying missionaries who brought us the gospel."

"I am sorry for my ignorance," I said, "but I didn't know there were Christians in the Orient then."

"There certainly were! Many of my countrymen responded with enthusiasm to the good news of our Lord. Even some of the great *daimyos*, or hereditary lords, became humble followers of Jesus Christ. The good news turned our whole world upside-down. We had lived in bondage to erroneous views of life, our world, and time for many generations. Individual lives had little meaning within the dominance of *karma*, or inexorable fate. One could only seek to live an honorable life in hopes of being acceptable to one's ancestors and find peace and release. We thought of time as a great wheel endlessly repeating itself. Good and evil were mirror opposites, locked in a perpetual and equal embrace. To learn about a Creator, the one God who made all things outside of and apart from himself, was a wonderful blessing. To learn that he is personal and good, and that 'good' has meaning, was like water to a thirsty soul. To find that he loves us, even in our sin, was enough to break one's heart with joy. That he sent his Son to suffer for us, to draw us to himself, made dying for him a privilege and a pleasure!"

"You died for him?" I asked, feeling humble in the presence of one of such spiritual fervor.

"Yes. The church in Japan was once strong and vibrant. Our witness was powerful and effective, and many changes occurred to improve the lives of us poor people. Yes, I was a poor man, a servant to a man of war. It was my earthly master, a *daimyo*, who rose in hatred against the church and led the great persecution. All who confessed to the name Christian were rounded up and penned together to starve, and many terribly tortured. Then, our oppressors decided that since we honor the memory of a crucified Man, we should follow his example. They nailed us to crosses by the hundreds. I was crucified next to a *samurai*, Tadasuke, a man who had once been a fearsome warrior, but who now had become a merciful, kind, and just leader. It was a great honor. Sadly, I have learned, the advance of the gospel was stopped in my country. The church in Japan dwindled to almost nothing, and was forced to go underground for many long years."

Who am I, I thought, to be seated next to one like this? I, whose greatest suffering was on the level of an overdrawn checkbook or algebra exam?

"I am ashamed, Gensuke," I said. "I never had to suffer for the name of Jesus. My life was easy."

"Do not feel ashamed, Daniel," he answered with a beaming smile. "To suffer or not to suffer was entirely in the hands of our sovereign God. He placed all of us in the place and time that pleased him, according to his purposes. To be faithful according to the stewardship one has received is the only important issue."

Have I been faithful? I wondered. I will find out soon.

I then had a sudden thought. "How have we been talking to one another, Gensuke? I don't know Japanese, and I assume you don't know English."

"I do not know, Daniel," he answered. "I have spoken to many here, from many times and places, and we have all communicated without difficulty."

I decided to ask Uriel the question, posing it in my mind. To my inner ear, he answered, "You are in the place where all communication was born. Your Lord is the living Word, remember. Do you recall the day of Pentecost, when all the gathered people heard the disciples glorifying God in their own languages? You have heard it called the gift of tongues. It was a temporary reversal of the judgment levied at the Tower of Babel, when God reduced the power of evil men by frustrating and dividing their speech. Pentecost was a preview of what you are now experiencing: all in Christ can understand and communicate to one another with perfect clarity. The judgment of divided tongues has ended, and all are unified in one speech."

Though all conversations in the arena were discreetly low, an audible hush fell over the millions now seated. I formed a question mark in my mind, and Uriel answered.

"The Lord approaches."

CHAPTER 10

~

Millions of redeemed people watched in silence as an angel in human form walked through a doorway at the back of the platform. He blazed with a silver fire, and was clothed in a deep blue robe marked with ornamental designs and bound with a silver girdle. He carried a large rod with a decorative head. I felt sure there was rich symbolic meaning in his garments and staff, and mentally noted to ask Uriel about them later.

For now, the angel commanded all attention. He took his position at the front of the platform and, raising his right hand, he struck the butt end of his staff three times on the ground with his left. Then, three times again. Then again. Three sets of three. Each blow made a sound like the loudest of thunder claps.

"Let all arise!" he cried. His voice sounded much like the one that announced the Lord's coming to earth. "Do honor to the Lord Jesus Christ, the Son of the living God, the Redeemer, the King of kings and Lord of lords!"

We rose to our feet, and stood with bowed heads in honor of the Lord. We waited in silence as he walked to the front of the platform, the angel moving to the side and bowing low. The angel straightened, and we took it as our cue to do the same.

The Lord was an awe-inspiring sight. Nothing could compare to the brightness of his glory. I had been impressed with the power evident in Uriel at our first meeting, but he was a pale imitation of the appearance of Christ. His glory was beyond description in earthly language. I understood now why the apostle John described his vision of the glorified Jesus in the terms he did: His face shining like the sun at full strength, and his eyes like flames of fire—even the seemingly odd description of a sword proceeding out of his mouth. The complete, irresistible authority of his spoken word struck my emotions with such force that a sword seemed an appropriate symbol. He was clothed in a robe that fell to his feet and bound with a golden girdle, representing the dignity of his priestly role. On his head was a crown (though I could not tell if he was wearing a literal crown, or if it was an impression made by his glorious appearance). All together, his garments proclaimed the union of his offices: Judge, Priest, and King.

"Welcome brethren and friends," said the Lord. "This is a day of judgment, honor, and glory. A day I have long anticipated, when I may honor my faithful witnesses, and reward those who have faithfully discharged their stewardships. It is fitting that we should do this before I conduct you to your new home in the heavenlies, the place I have prepared for you. This is the occasion for my bride, the Church whom I love, to make herself ready and to be clothed in fine linen, to become a wonder at which all who live on earth or in the heavens will marvel."

The Lord stood in silence for a moment, then continued. "Let us honor my Father, who will witness these proceedings." He turned and stood facing the empty section of the arena.

Over the rim of the stadium in that direction appeared a moving light, brighter than anything I had ever seen. As it descended and moved closer, I began to make out a shape. It was roughly a cube, with odd-shaped projections at the corners. It glowed as if made of pure, blinding light, silver and golden, and seemed to have moving parts at its interior. Above the object, there seemed to be a flat, smooth expanse. Nothing in my experience helped me to recognize what I was seeing. There were moving parts apparently within moving parts, confusing my senses. Backing off with my vision, I realized that the projections on the corners were angelic beings that were actually bearing the object. These angels wore forms unlike anything I had ever seen, almost projecting an appearance of winged man-like beasts. My memory clicked, and I remembered: This must be what the prophet Ezekiel saw. Ezekiel's vision of the glory of God in the Bible always seemed to me completely bizarre. Now I understood why he could not describe the sight in earthly terms. There is no way to do so. One could only struggle with language heavily weighted with hedges and disclaimers.

They were much closer now, nearly above the amphitheater. With all eyes on them, the angelic bearers began crying out: "Holy, holy, holy, is the Lord of hosts: all creation is full of his glory." A gasp arose from the assembled multitude, and we hastily fell to our knees and bowed low.

We were visited by the manifest presence of the living God.

I had heard all my life about the promise of seeing God, never thinking much about what that would mean. I never thought seriously about the trembling of my heart or the depths of holy fear I could feel. How could I—a believer who should have known better—have ever laughed at a joke involving the living God? How could I have ever used his name without meaning, or worse, as a curse? Many worldly people talk as if it would be a lark to come face to face with God our Creator. The reality of the experience shook every fiber and nerve in my body. What will become of those on earth who flippantly speak of "The Man Upstairs" or "The Big Guy"?

I lifted my gaze to see the Lord's glory descend to a spot in that open area behind the Bema. The angelic beings continued to cry out:

> Holy, holy, holy, is the Lord God Almighty, which was, and is, and is to come. All creation is full of his glory. The heavens are yours, the earth also is yours: as for the world and its fullness, you have founded them. Righteousness and justice are the foundation of your throne. Mercy and truth go before you. Blessed are the people that know the joyful sound: they shall walk, O Lord, in the light of your countenance. In your name shall they rejoice all the day: and in your righteousness shall they be exalted.

At some point in the crying of the heralds, I found myself joining with the multitude in the doxology, praising God in unison. Just as on our arrival in the heavenlies, the Holy Spirit was moving us and directing our worship. With one heart and one voice we gave honor to our God and Father.

A Voice—and that term is far too insipid for the spoken words that emanated from above the expanse—replied, with a thunderous tone that sounded as if it would shake the universe:

> I Am Who I Am. I Am He Who Is. I Am
> He Who Is God. I am compassionate and
> gracious, longsuffering and slow to anger,
> abundant in mercy, lovingkindness and
> truth. I keep mercy for thousands, forgiv-
> ing iniquity and transgression and sin. Yet
> I will by no means clear the guilty or let
> them go unpunished.

We responded with a great song to the praise of God's grace:

> The Lord is merciful and gracious, slow to
> anger, and full of compassion. He will not
> always strive with sinful men: neither will
> he keep his anger forever. He has not dealt
> with us according to our sins; nor re-
> warded us according to our iniquities. For
> as the heavens are high above the earth, so
> great is his mercy toward them that fear
> him. As far as the east is from the west, so

far has he removed our transgressions from
us. Praise the Lord!

His love is abundant, his holiness is
pure. His forgiveness is free, yet purchased
at great cost. His righteousness has been
honored, for in forgiving men he made no
compromise with evil. He judged sin entirely through the substitution of his Son,
the Lamb of God who takes away the sin
of the world, and his justice was satisfied.
He justifies the ungodly; he forgives the
sinner; he ransoms the enslaved; he recon-
ciles his enemy; he sanctifies the stranger.
All honor is his! All glory is his! We thank
you, and praise your name forever and
ever!

This was another occasion when I lost all comprehension of time passing. I can't tell you if we worshipped for
minutes, hours, or days.

Previously, whenever I thought about seeing God, I
tended to have a vague mental picture of a manlike figure
on a throne. If you had actually asked me what it meant to
see God, I had enough theological knowledge to know that
my mental image could not be literally true. I knew that
God is a Spirit, without physical form or structure. A God
who is omnipresent could not be confined to a body or location. Most biblical accounts of a prophet or apostle seeing God seemed to me strange, confusing, or vague.

Now I knew why. My theology was correct. God is an
omnipresent Spirit, not confined to a body or limits of any

kind. How can you see One who is omnipresent—as present beyond the farthest galaxy as he is near you? You cannot see him in his entirety, only a manifest (or revealed) local presence. The same Bible that says we shall see God also describes him as the God "no man has seen nor can see"—an apparent contradiction. Now, seeing probably the same appearance that was revealed to Ezekiel (and possibly also to others, like Isaiah, Daniel, and John), I understood. The God of Israel was always—uniquely in the ancient idolatrous world—the God without an image. Even the sacred Ark of the Covenant was only a representation of the foundation of his throne. It was, in fact, a representation of what I was now seeing.

And yet ... and yet, I can say that I saw God! There is no way to describe it in earthly language and categories. It is as if I were granted a sixth sense. How can you explain sight to a blind man or hearing to a deaf man? How can I explain a new sixth sense given to the transformed saints to enable us to comprehend the presence of God? I cannot.

The Lord Jesus continued to stand as we worshipped the Father. At length, he bowed his head for a moment. He looked up, raised his arms, and all fell silent. He spoke: "I thank you, Father, for these whom you have given me, all whose names are recorded in the book of life. They are yours, and you have given them to me. After they have been examined and rewarded, I will present them back to you, that they may forever be trophies of your grace. May they love you and serve you forever, even as I have loved you and served you. Glorify your name."

Again, the Voice came from above the expanse over the throne. "I have glorified it, and I will glorify it again. Welcome, my children, beloved of mine and of my Son.

Now is the time for judgment to begin, but I do not judge. I have committed all judgment to my Son, that all should honor the Son, even as they honor the Father. Proceed."

The Lord Jesus turned to face us, and said, "Be seated."

He stood facing the millions in the arena. "You will each be called in turn to come and be examined."

My eyes widened in astonishment as I considered what that meant. There are hundreds of millions here! It is a good thing, I thought, that time is elastic (using Uriel's term) here in the heavenlies!

"Judgment will be conducted according to these criteria. First, according to quality. Upon the foundation of faith in me you have built your lives. What sort of building materials you have chosen will become evident as they are tested by the fire of truth. Second, according to your stewardship. It is required of a steward that he be found faithful. The judgment will not compare you one to another. It will be according to the gifts, time, and opportunities granted to you, and to you alone. Third, according to motives. Man looks at the outward appearance, but God looks on the heart. I will look not only at what you have done, but why you have done it.

"The result of the judgment shall be reward. While all will be glorified in me, there are varying degrees of glory. Those who have honored me, I will honor. Those who proved faithful in little things will be granted responsibility in great matters. Stewards who proved faithful to me in their own lives will be given authority over others. Some will serve as rulers of cities, some of provinces, some of nations.

"There will also be special awards. The Crown of Righteousness to those who looked faithfully for me and loved my appearing. The Crown of Life for those who fulfilled the greatest of the commandments, who loved me with purity and sincerity. The Crown of Glory for those faithful undershepherds who pastored my flock in my name. The Crown of Life, again, for those who endured suffering and persecution for the sake of my name. And the Crown of Faith, for those who have persevered under trial and remained faithful to the end."

The Lord Jesus looked all around the massive crowd filling the stadium. "Let us begin," he said. He turned, walked back to the throne at the center of the platform, and sat down. To the angel he said, "Call to me the first of the saints."

CHAPTER 11

The blue clad angel turned to the assembly and struck the platform three times with his staff. "Timolaus Germanicus of Lugdunum," he cried.

Immediately, a saint flew to the floor of the stadium, landing beneath the Bema (whether under his own power or with angelic assistance, I do not know). He stood for a moment, then walked up the steps. Watching him, I nearly felt his holy fear. How could *anyone* approach him who sat there? In the back of my mind, I counted the steps as he climbed: There were ten. The crowd was completely silent.

He reached the top of the platform and stood still, apparently awaiting a command. The Lord spoke to him, and he walked to within a few feet of the throne. Though I could not hear the words, I could see him speak a few sentences to which Timolaus nodded. This part of the judgment was obviously meant to be private.

At the same time, I received another surprise. Into my mind flashed knowledge ... information ... almost a

biographical sketch of Timolaus. I didn't know for certain
the source of this knowledge, but I felt somehow it was
coming from the angelic herald.

I knew that this saint had lived in what we called the
third century, in an area which later became known as
Lyon, France. It was part of the Roman Empire in a time
of great trial for the church. One of the worst of all persecutions was waged against Christians, under the orders of
the Emperor Decius. Timolaus was one of the many faithful martyrs who gave their lives for their faith. A poor man,
a smith by trade, he had served as a deacon, one who over-
saw and distributed gifts to the poor. He had often given of
his own meager means to feed others who were hungry.
Because he refused to renounce Christ and swear allegiance to Caesar through an act of worship, he had been
subjected to numerous tortures. He had been "scraped."
That means the flesh had been torn from his body by the
application of sharp instruments made from seashells. He
had been stretched on the rack. Finally, his mangled body,
still living, had been cast into the arena to be devoured by
lions and leopards. To the end, throughout the tortures
and in the arena, his only cry had been, "My name is
Timolaus. I am a Christian!"

My heart broke as this knowledge came into my mind.
The suffering this saint had endured took my breath away.
His courage and faith made my heart feel as if it would
burst in my breast. This man is my brother! It is *my brother*
who has suffered thus for Christ's sake.

The entire judgment, as I experienced time passing,
took only a few moments. There was nothing much to see.
Whatever was going on between the Lord and Timolaus
on that platform was between them alone. Suddenly,

Timolaus collapsed. He fell to his knees, then on his face. He appeared utterly undone.

Then the most amazing thing happened. The Lord Jesus rose from his seat. He strode the few steps to the prostrate figure, knelt and touched him, raising him to his feet. With his hands on the saint's shoulders, the Lord said to him the words every member of the assembly longed to hear: "Well done, good and faithful servant!"

There was a blinding flash, and Timolaus was transformed into a creature of beauty and glory that surpasses my powers of description. He was made like our Lord, his face gleaming like the sun. There appeared around his head crowns—though like the Lord's, I could not tell if he was wearing literal objects. I am inclined to think that the impression of crowns was really facets or aspects of glory (I can think of no better words), which augmented his glorified appearance. I knew intuitively that Timolaus had been awarded the Crown of Life and the Crown of Faith.

Most remarkable of all was the glory of his appearance. On earth, we were all largely facades. We judged one another by attractiveness, social status, education, clothing, grammar, manners—all those foolish external ways of evaluating people. Here in the heavenlies we are going to see people as they really are: as God sees them. What is in their hearts, the real worth of a person, will correspond completely with the glory seen on the outside. Again, my breath faltered at the sight of this saint's beauty and glory. However his contemporaries judged him, the truth was now known: Timolaus was a truly great soul who loved the Lord with all his heart and loved others for his sake.

The Lord turned him by the shoulders to face the crowd, and stood at his side with one hand on his back.

"This is my beloved Timolaus Germanicus, in whom I am well pleased."

The shouts and cheers were deafening. They were equal parts cries of welcome, words of honor, and gasps of astonishment. With evident joy, Timolaus flew back to his seat in the arena, like a meteor streaking through the heavens. The whole stadium seemed to rumble and quake with excitement. For me, I cannot begin to describe the love I felt for him, for my brother in Christ. We had never met, nor had I ever heard of him before. But now I knew him, and knew him truly. Of course, in the future we could become personally acquainted, and there will be much to learn and appreciate. I looked forward to the experience. At that moment, however, seeing him in his glorified state, I knew that I saw him as he truly is, and I was overwhelmed with love and awe.

And Timolaus Germanicus of Lugdunum was only the *first* of the saints to be examined! The Lord returned to his throne and nodded to the herald. The angel struck his staff on the platform three times and cried, "Chang T'ai Tsung." Another saint flew to the floor and deliberately ascended the steps. This was a Christian from thirteenth century China, during a time of toleration when the Khan dynasty ruled.

As he approached the Bema, I asked, "Uriel, how is it that I am receiving knowledge about these as they approach the judgment?"

"I presume, Sir, that the Lord wants you to know a little more about one another than what you see here. Remember: the judgment is not only about what each one has done, but what each has done on the basis of what he has received. All are not given the same time, gifts, or opportunities, so the judgment must take those things into account."

"From where is the knowledge coming?" I asked.

"From the great herald himself, Kolael, whose name means 'Voice of God.' It is he you see standing on the platform. I presume as well that you may seek answers or more information from him if you wish. Simply apply your will to your question, and address it to him as you would to me."

I tried Uriel's suggestion and found he was right. As individuals came forward for judgment, I was curious about and interested in all of them. By posing my questions, I found I could receive mental pictures of the life and works of the saint on the platform. As in our first time of worship in the heavenlies, I felt no sense of fatigue or boredom. On the contrary, I never in all my existence felt so intensely interested in or stimulated about anything as I was each individual saint as he stood before our Lord.

Obviously, I cannot describe very many of the individual judgments. They would have taken centuries of earth's time to conduct, even at only a minute or two apiece. There were billions of saints to be examined. I must therefore share only general observations and accounts of a few examples.

Each of the individual judgments followed roughly the same pattern and time span. The few private words of the Lord in the beginning. Occasionally the saint would speak, presumably to ask or answer a question. After a short time, the saint was overcome. Some wobbled on their feet; others sank to their knees in apparent exhaustion; some fell as if unconscious, totally prostrate on the platform. The Lord would then touch them, raising them to their feet, and introduce him or her to the assembled multitude.

Here also differences were apparent. Not all received the commendation, "Well done, good and faithful servant." Not all heard the words, "in whom I am well pleased." All were indeed glorified. As the judgments progressed, however, it became obvious what the Lord meant by "degrees of glory." An appearance of the least of the glorified saints would have blinded earthly eyes. The least of the saints represented a true image of our Lord. But there were levels of glory that transcended others. There were, sad to say, saints that entered the heavenlies spiritually bankrupt. They proved to have accomplished nothing of value with the deposit of eternal life they had been given. Or, they had begun well, only to have turned later from the pursuit of Christ and had been disqualified for rewards. We were not told the details of why a person's life was reckoned as so much wood, hay, and straw. We saw only the result.

We loved those bankrupt saints no less. They were welcomed back into the assembly with joy, compassion, and love. There was no envy, competition, or jealousy in the heavenlies. All are as they should be, and all are willing servants of our Lord, whatever the station of honor. If anything, seeing these brothers and sisters fail to win the race of faith only hardened our hearts against sin as we saw more of its results. I felt I understood better what Uriel meant when he described watching me wrestle with temptation. He had said it only made him hate evil and sin all the more. I was beginning to feel the same.

There were relatively few, however, who lost all their rewards. After all, it was the Lord Jesus who had said that he would remember even a cup of cold water given in his name. In his grace, he found something commendable in almost all his people—often something that surprised the recipient above all. The rewards given to those who faithfully persevered graded up to degrees of glory beyond description. The best I can do would be to use the comparison of beautiful gemstones. One diamond looks dazzlingly beautiful, until it is compared side by side with another. The second has been cut more carefully with many more facets. It thus possesses a brilliance that surpasses the first. Add aspects of color and fire, and each gem becomes a unique work of art. In the heavenlies, every saint is an individual work of the great Artist himself. The difference in this case being that the object has a participatory role in his development. He can cooperate with the Artist, or resist—even frustrate—the process of his development.

Watching the progress of the judgment, certain thoughts continued to rebound in my mind: Life really mattered! Our choices and actions really mattered! Life was not just a game. It wasn't just a place to have the most fun. We were making choices—choosing courses of action, setting priorities, becoming someone—that had eternal ramifications.

Always in the back of my mind was the knowledge that my time was coming. What will the Lord make of *my* choices?

CHAPTER 12

⸙

What a joy it was to be freed from earthly limitations! As time (by whatever measure we were experiencing it) passed, I felt complete liberty from fatigue, boredom, or restlessness. Millions of individual believers went forward to be judged and returned to their places as glorified saints. I could discern no order or reason for the sequence in which people were called. It was not according to achievement, class, nation, or time in history. The Lord alone knew.

It would naturally be impossible to tell many stories. It would be impossible to tell even one story in real detail. Neither can I pick my favorites or the most interesting. They were all my favorites, and all were the most interesting. How can you judge between truly unique things? Every glorified saint can almost be described as a species unto himself. I found myself continually surprised and delighted at the incredible variety and span of the Church of

Jesus Christ. To give you an idea, here are a few sketches in
no particular order.

Early in the proceedings, Teresa of Mexico City was
called, and a saint flew to the platform. This was a judgment unlike the first several I had seen, but only the beginning of multitudes more like it. Kolael was silent about this
individual. After the initial conversation between the Lord
and Teresa and the usual intervening moments, the Lord
Jesus arose and walked over to her. Unlike others, Teresa
did not show signs of a devastatingly powerful examina-
tion. She stood straight and tall as the Lord placed his
hands on her shoulders, looked her in the eye, and spoke
some private words to her. There was a flash, and Teresa
was transformed into a glorious figure unlike others we
had seen. She shined with a purity and beauty that was remarkable, even with all we had already witnessed. Hers
was a beauty of a new type. Simple I would call it, or un-
complicated, crystal clear and brilliant.

I directed a question at Kolael and he enlightened me.
Teresa was one who had died in early childhood. She had
indeed come to believe in Jesus Christ, but she had little
chance to grow, live, or make choices on earth. While no
children of Adam are born without the inherited stain of
original sin, Teresa, like many millions of others, had died
long before committing much willful sin of her own. She
never gained much understanding of moral responsibility.
Though she had died as a small child on earth, she was here
a fully developed adult. She had not had the opportunity
to earn rewards through earthly service, but neither did she
have the awful experience of committing sins of her own,
of bearing the scars of evil on her soul. Resurrected saints
like Teresa will begin their heavenly existence with the

purity of the innocent (realizing that "innocent" is a relative term—only Jesus was truly innocent in human history), with the opportunity to grow in wisdom and beauty forever. I breathed a prayer of praise and thanksgiving to God for his wonderful mercy and kindness.

I thought of another question. "Uriel, what of all those who died as infants? There must have been millions of them, who never had any chance to accept or reject the Lord. What will happen to them?"

"I am unfortunately not permitted to answer that question," Uriel replied. "Rest assured that the Lord has an answer which is in full harmony with his holy character and overarching mercy. But until he has chosen to announce it, it must remain sealed."

"Then I will wait until he is ready to do so," I answered, confident of the Lord's wisdom and love. At the same time, it was sobering to think of all those infants and children who never had the opportunity to serve the Lord. If much is required of those to whom much is given, what will I have to show for my full and advantaged life?

Ho Ga Qua, a Mohawk of the seventeenth century, came forward. He learned the gospel from a Puritan settler in New England, and adopted the name Peter Smith when dealing with the settlers. Ho Ga Qua became an outstanding evangelist among his native people, and later served as pastor of a Mohawk village that was mostly Christian. After two decades of faithfully serving the Lord, he was killed in a misguided retaliatory raid by settlers after a renegade Algonquin band had attacked some whites. He received the Crown of Glory among other honors for faithfully shepherding the Lord's people.

Pomponia Graecina was a high-born Roman woman of the first century. In fact, as far as I can tell, she was the first Roman of the senatorial class to become a Christian. Sometime in the 50s—even before Paul arrived in Rome—she was genuinely converted, and sincerely pursued her faith. She became the subject of gossip among her peers, to whom "embracing a foreign superstition" was a scandal. To protect her from gossip and attack, her husband, Plautius, conducted a "family tribunal," an old Roman custom that was nearly out-of-date by that time. In a family tribunal, the head of the house convened a family court, and placed a member on trial. In traditional Roman practice, the sanctity of the home was such that acquittal in a family tribunal ended any public dispute. Pomponia was cleared of charges by her husband, and she went on to practice her faith quietly for the rest of her life. Plautius was converted, too, shortly before he died, and their home was still being used by Christians as a meeting place a century later.

Kairaba Saloum was born in the Gold Coast, West Africa near the end of the nineteenth century. He took the Christian name, Daniel, and applied the high intelligence God had given him to learning the Scriptures, memorizing approximately half the Bible. He served as a teacher and evangelist among his people, becoming a small part of what was possibly the greatest wave of evangelism in all church history. I was amazed to learn of the millions of people converted in Africa in the twentieth century, having been ignorant even of their existence. But I was ignorant no longer. Millions and millions of African Christians were in attendance. Many had endured great hardship for the name of Jesus, and many were highly honored saints.

Oswald of Kent, in Anglo-Saxon Britain, lived in the eighth century. He was desperately poor, a blacksmith's assistant, scratching out day-to-day barely enough for him and his family to live on. He never learned to read or write, but he loved the Lord. From his local priest, who himself was barely literate, he learned the outlines of the gospel. He memorized any scraps of Holy Scripture he heard from any source. Though he owned almost nothing, living in a hovel made of rock and clay, he still shared food and shelter with others, many times giving away his single daily meal. Most importantly, he developed a relationship with Jesus Christ that was intimate to a degree I hardly knew was possible on earth. He truly practiced Paul's injunction to pray without ceasing. Oswald was one of the most highly honored saints.

The call of Fanny Crosby elicited a gush of pleasure from the observers. Though I was somewhat familiar with Fanny due to her many famous hymns, Kolael told me much more. Here was one who began life with a series of tragedies, as people commonly view things. And yet, she went on to enjoy a full, happy, and fruitful life for the Lord. As an infant, Fanny was blinded for life by the treatment of an incompetent doctor, then her father died. With her mother working as a maid to make a bare living, Fanny was reared by her godly grandmother.

As a young girl, she applied her excellent mind to learning the Scriptures, memorizing up to five chapters a week. As a teenager, Fanny entered a school for the blind, where she went on to teach for many years. An accomplished pianist, singer, and poet, it was natural that Fanny should compose songs. By the time she completed her life at age ninety-five, she had written over eight thousand songs which first were popularized through the evangelistic crusades of Dwight L. Moody, and which continued to be loved and used until the present.

Fanny's heart of joy and love for her Savior was the secret behind her music's popularity. She never allowed herself to fall into self-pity over her blindness. She would reply to sympathetic comments, "My blindness has been a great blessing!. How else could my life have been so beneficial?" On one occasion, a minister expressed his regret that Fanny did not have sight to go along with her evident gifts. "Don't be sorry," replied Fanny. "If God had given me the choice before my birth, I would have asked to be born blind." When the surprised pastor asked why, she replied, "Because when I get to heaven, the first sight my eyes shall ever see will be my Jesus!" Now at the Bema, Fanny was granted her deepest desire.

Hrolf Sigurdson had been a wild barbarian, chief of a marauding Viking band who ranged from their native Denmark to western Europe spreading terror and death. On murderous raids to England, he had personally split the skulls of several others that were in attendance at the Bema! In the middle of the ninth century, he heard the gospel from a captured Saxon monk that he had intended to execute. He was so disturbed by the conversation that he ran away into the wilderness for three nights. After spending a night in a drunken rage, he knelt facing the sun as it rose over the North Sea and asked the Lord Jesus to come into his heart and save him. He chose to remain in England and settled down, with many of his former bandits following his example. He became a kind, giving, and faithful man, who worked with the local abbot to serve and teach the people of his village. To the end of his days, he lived in deep repentance for his former ways, yet was full of joy, knowing the forgiveness of the Lord.

Basil of Caesarea lived in the fourth century. He had joined the early ascetic movement in Syria, living in isolation for years, starving and abusing his body. I must admit that I found it difficult to relate to the desert ascetics like Basil, though his zeal for the Lord was unquestioned. His flight to the desert seemed chiefly motivated by two things: his disgust with the compromising, worldly church of that time; and his own unquenchable thirst to know the Lord Jesus. Here was a good example of God looking on the heart of his people, while men look at the outward appearance. Many of the ascetics were confused in theology, and many wasted their efforts aiming at goals God never specified. The Lord, however, always sees the real heart within, and he richly rewarded Basil for the genuine and intense love he had for God.

Basil calls to mind one of the great lessons I learned at the Bema: that a saint's heart may be right even while his head is confused. I lived in an age with abundant information, learning opportunities on every hand, and sound teaching. I must have had eight or ten Bibles in my home (gathering dust, too often). Here with the assembled Church of all history, I realized how rare my experience had been. I took for granted my access to the Word of God, and as so often happens, familiarity bred contempt (or, at least, complacency). Millions of saints who lived before the invention of the printing press did not even understand the basics of the gospel clearly! Millions never held a Bible in their hands. Many never heard John 3:16, which thousands of pre-school children in my time could recite with ease. For millions, information about Jesus Christ, the Savior of the world, was perceived only through a confused haze of ignorance, symbolism, and superstition. God, however, always looked on the heart of men, and he was always looking for the response of faith. Where someone desired to know the truth and be reconciled to God, he was always able to communicate the knowledge of himself to them—even to those who could never have passed an exam on their theological understanding. I began to see how blessed I had been to have lived in a time with abundant access to the Holy Scriptures, to sound doctrinal teaching of the Word, and with the political liberty to pursue my faith. Why had I not taken more advantage of those opportunities?

During the judgment of one Antonia Romula, a woman of Phrygia, I learned of an astonishing incident. Around the end of the third century, nearly her entire city in what is now northern Turkey converted to Christ. Rare for that time, members of every social strata, including the city council members and the local governor, became Christians. During the terrible persecution ordered by the Emperor Diocletian, the city was surrounded and besieged by a Roman garrison. By Imperial order, almost the entire population of the town was slaughtered because they would not offer pagan sacrifices. A whole Christian city martyred at a stroke! Antonia had taken many believers into her home, choosing to stay and suffer with other Christians rather than fleeing when she had the chance, and died with them.

By no means have all Christians been persecuted or martyred for their faith, but many, many more than I ever knew had been. Many more of my brothers and sisters in Christ suffered terribly for the name of Jesus than I ever dreamed. That doesn't mean they were super Christians.

Not even dying for the Faith guaranteed that one was more highly honored than others. As Gensuke had said, whether or not one suffered for Christ's sake was a matter determined by our Sovereign God. Another martyred saint told me during a later conversation, "I promise you: we would have gladly avoided suffering if we could have. But we were willing to endure if it was the will of God."

For one like me, it was eye-opening, sobering, and incredibly humbling to learn how costly it has been throughout much of history simply to bear the name, Christian. The love of some of these saints for God and for one another was incredible. Near the end of the first century, for example, many believing men and women actually sold themselves into slavery to purchase food for other needy saints or to redeem others out of slavery. I wondered: When have I ever loved someone that much? When have I ever quit thinking of myself and my desires long enough to become even dimly *aware* of others and their needs?

I have said nothing about denominations, because they were irrelevant at this point. Irrelevant, that is, except as additional raw materials for the judgment—more details of the stewardship each has received from God. Now, however, with Christ the living Word on the throne before them, past disputes between groups were no longer the issue. That is not to say that all denominations were equal in accuracy, achievement, or health. God is a God of truth, and mutually contradictory assertions about God, the Word, or the gospel cannot both be true. At least one party in all disputes must have been wrong. Sometimes both or all were wrong. All were wrong at least some of the time. Disputes sometimes stemmed from honest disagreement held with integrity by sincere hearts. Other times, believers were morally responsible for the errors they believed and taught. Their personal agendas or intellectual dishonesty steered them to beliefs and assertions that were self-serving or convenient.

From the perspective of the Bema, I could see what a great advantage and blessing the knowledge of biblical truth was in daily living. It was the Lord himself who had said, "If you continue in my word, then are you my disciples indeed; and you shall know the truth, and the truth shall make you free." If it is truth that sets people free, then the opposite is also true: It is error, ignorance, or lies that hold people in bondage. History is full of examples of people kept in spiritual bondage through erroneous ideas about God and his Word. Here is another example of the importance of having access to the Bible. Only those who could learn authoritative truth from the Word for themselves had any defense against spiritual domination. It was personal study of the Bible by men like Martin Luther and Ulrich Zwingli that led to the great Reformation, as well as to lesser reform movements throughout history. Of course, there were always those who misused or twisted the Scriptures to their own and others' detriment, either because they were mentally or emotionally unstable, or because they were driven by the sins of their flesh. Here at the Bema, the Lord was sorting out which was which.

Members of every Christian denomination were represented. In fact, there were many who had been members of pseudo-Christian cults on earth, such as the Gnostics and Manichaeans in the early centuries, or Mormons and Jehovah's Witnesses in later years. None had been saved through the erroneous teaching of the cults, but in spite of them. Many of these were believers who had later been deceived and seduced into joining the cults. Others had grown up in cult families, but had been given the grace to ignore or see through the cult's teachings and perceive the real nature of Jesus Christ. As always, the Lord was looking chiefly for hearts of contrition and faith. As the Good Shepherd, he sought his lost sheep, and found them in what would seem to us some of the most unlikely places.

For many, the Bema was their occasion to know God's answer to the great unanswered question of life on earth: the "why" of suffering. Whether people suffered outright persecution or suffered from natural sources—such as diseases, injuries, deformities, hunger, poverty, or the death of loved ones—all was made clear by the Lord. The complexities of God's wisdom and plan proved to be beyond even glorified human comprehension. Someone's life was spared to ensure that a particular baby was born. A soldier died in battle so that a different man's line would continue. A woman miscarried to enable another baby to be conceived. One suffered affliction so an observer could learn of God's grace. A man might be disciplined for a sin to protect him from committing a greater sin.

Perhaps most amazing: Over and over we saw that, while never the author of evil, God often used the evil of men for his own purposes, as raw materials to bring about a greater good. Whatever the situation, all learned to bow before God's sovereign will and agree that his decrees were good and right. No one left the Bema dissatisfied. Each discovered the reality of God's promise to cause all things to work together for good to those who love him and are called according to his purpose.

As I watched the progress of the judgments, I could see where God's sovereign plan touched my life. In the first decade of the twentieth century, a family named Nelson immigrated to Minnesota from their native Norway. After a few years in America, the matriarch of the family became terribly homesick, and persuaded her husband to go back home. After a short time in Norway, she decided that her idyllic memory of the old country was faulty, so they packed up to return to America. The Nelsons sailed toward Southampton, England, planning to transfer to another ship bound for the New World, but they missed their connection by fifteen minutes and had to wait some time for another ship. What a disappointment! Except that the ship they missed by fifteen minutes was the *Titanic*.

Sixteen months later, having settled in the Seattle area, Momma Nelson gave birth to a son. That boy grew up, and became the father of three daughters. One of those girls grew up, and became the mother of a daughter, Susan, whom I married.

As I thought of my wife and three children, I saw how a difference in fifteen minutes could have changed everything. Their lives may not have existed. Mine would have been totally different. To think of how God has spun the web of human history to bring about exactly the people and events he desired was miles beyond my mental capacity. The only thing I could do in response was bow in worship and adoration.

If there was anything all were now fully aware of, it was that they were saved completely by the unmerited grace of God through faith in Jesus Christ. Any confusion about this fact was completely cured by the time one stood before the glorified Savior. No one left the platform with misconceptions about any merit he or she might have contributed to their salvation. Salvation was an undeserved gift of God received by faith alone.

Even rewards were also, at base, gifts of grace. I remembered the scene from Revelation where the elders cast their crowns before the throne of God. Whether that was a metaphor or will be literally fulfilled, the meaning is the same. Yes, it pleased the Lord Jesus to grant crowns and degrees of glory to his people, but every observer was clear on one fact: All glory, honor, and praise truly and ultimately belonged only to him, who loved us and delivered himself over to death on our behalf.

CHAPTER 13

．ぐ・

As the judgments progressed, my concentration and interest never wavered. Most of the saints, of course, I had never heard of on earth. I had read a few history books in my life, but now I could see how sketchy and out of proportion they were, at best, and how outright erroneous they were, at worst. At the Judgment Seat of Christ, we were seeing God's real history as he saw it. My education continued.

It has been said that histories are written by the victors, and I learned that the saying is true. The majority of the most significant and godly saints of two millennia were totally unnoticed or forgotten on earth. Often, it was because they were the "losers" in worldly conflicts—at least by human estimation. Throughout many dark periods when the professing church was in the hands of ungodly, evil, worldly men, there were wonderful believers living godly, saintly lives. Those who kept quiet or appeared harmless to the establishment sometimes got to live out their days in anonymity. Those who protested the wrongs of the institutional church or, worse, tried to bring reform, often were snuffed out. In either case, they seldom rated a mention in written records. Besides, it was rarely good, normal people who made news. Villains always got the lion's share of the press. Common dictators and conquerors like Alexander or Napoleon, responsible for death and destruction on a massive scale, called forth volumes of scholarly tomes, while truly great saints who will blaze with the glory of God through all eternity were forgotten by their own descendants.

I was intrigued by the story of one Maria of Milan. She joined the Humiliati movement in the twelfth century, which later merged with a group known as the Waldenses. These were believers who, in reaction against the church of the time, sought a return to the pure New Testament faith by imitating Jesus as literally as possible. They dressed in robes and sandals, forsook wealth, and traveled two by two throughout the countryside working with their hands and preaching a simple gospel. In addition, the Humiliati and Waldenses took a position rare during the Middle Ages that women and laymen were competent to preach and teach. Maria joined them enthusiastically. After a number of scrapes with the authorities and several near-arrests, however, Maria fled with many of her companions to the far reaches of the Alps, where the movement continued in obscurity for several more centuries. History books focus on the activities of the "victorious" institutional "church" during those centuries, while simple believers lived quiet lives in out-of-the-way places without notice. Without notice, that is, except for the Lord's notice, which is the one that really counted.

It was exciting, certainly, to see the apostles at the Bema. Peter, Paul, John, and the others felt familiar as family while we were still on earth. Seeing them in person here, we felt as if they were heroic elder brothers. It was thrilling. Even apostles, though, were judged according to the stewardship they had been given. They were honored for faithfully discharging the unique offices they held. They had each suffered for the Name and were appropriately rewarded, as they were for shepherding the Lord's flock. And, they will hold unique positions as judges when the Lord's kingdom is inaugurated on earth. But holding the office of apostle was not in itself reason for greater glory than that bestowed on other saints.

Neither was it an advantage to have been a pastor or other church officer. These, in fact, were judged more strictly, because of the influence they wielded over others. Plus, there were widely varying roles for those who led the Church. A pastor might be called upon to shepherd a flock of Christians in a time of fierce persecution. In such a situation, his main job might have been simply to encourage the believers to stand firm in the Faith, and to see that people were fed and clothed until he himself was martyred. Most of the names in this category had passed into historical oblivion on earth. Or, a pastor might have been called to be a scholar and orator, proclaiming the Word of God in a setting of relative freedom and peace. Tens of thousands had their lives touched by the biblical preaching of Whitefield and Spurgeon, for example. Or, a pastor might be called to shepherd a small group in an obscure rural or frontier location, marrying, burying, and loving his people as he accompanied them through the transitions of life.

Few of these were heard of outside their vicinities, and fewer remembered even there.

God, however, always remembered. It reminded me of the military, where one's primary responsibility is to man his post until relieved. The Lord did not judge the various ministers of his Church against one another, but by their faithfulness to man their post. The other principle that came into play was the one the Lord had taught: "To whom much is given, much is required." Once again, it proved to be a matter of stewardship.

Many big names from the history books were at the Bema, and it was interesting to observe them in person. It was very different, though, from our earthly experience with celebrities. A celebrity was someone who was famous for being famous. In the heavenlies, glory was the reality of what someone was in the estimation of God. Fame had nothing to do with it. Those who were famous on earth sometimes were worthy of great glory in heaven, and sometimes they were not.

Another of the lessons I learned: God did not require perfect instruments to accomplish His work in the world. Some of the saints who made a great impact for the Lord had glaring blind spots.

From the early centuries, Origen was one example. His zeal was so great that as a young man he *pursued* martyrdom. After his father was killed for being a Christian, Origen sought to follow him, desiring to die for his faith as well. He was saved on that occasion only because his mother hid his clothes and he was too ashamed to go outside without them! Later, he founded a school which, unusual for the time, admitted female students. To teach and disciple them safely without the temptations and dangers of lust, he castrated himself—taking literally the Lord's words about becoming a eunuch for the kingdom of God. Oddly, in one who would make so drastic a decision based on a literal understanding of the Scriptures, he became known for advocating an allegorical, or symbolic, approach to biblical interpretation. While Origen was very influential as a theologian and his personal godliness was widely known and respected, his allegorizing methods also unwittingly set the stage for many serious errors that plagued the Church to the end of her history. Nevertheless, Origen was a highly honored saint at the Bema. His heart of love and faith burned brightly, despite his flawed understanding.

William Carey stood out as an ordinary saint who made a massive impact for Christ, a truly unlikely hero. Though only a poor shoemaker, in the eighteenth century he was as responsible as anyone for the birth of the modern missionary movement. His desire to obey and serve God was total, as was his dedication to do what he believed God commanded. Like every Christian, his performance fell far short of his aspirations. And yet, despite his faults, Carey was used by God to stab awake a complacent Church, and change the whole world through the thousands of others he influenced to do the same. Millions heard the gospel and received eternal life because this saint, branded a screwball by his generation of Christians, tried sincerely to obey God's call to take the good news to the world. Millions at the Bema watched his judgment with unspeakable gratitude, for their salvation was a direct result (humanly speaking) of his service. The heat of William Carey's dedication rebuked my cold, arrogant heart.

Following his evaluation, the Lord turned Carey to face the crowd. "William," he said, "behold your harvest!" I don't know exactly what Carey himself saw, but somehow the Lord opened his eyes to see the millions of individuals among the watchers whose lives in time and eternity were transformed through God's use of this humble human instrument. What a moment it must have been for him!

I had no unusual interest at first in the saint the herald summoned as "Aurelius Augustinus" until I realized that this was the person known throughout the world as Saint Augustine. His judgment struck me as particularly memorable, because he was one whose great earthly renown seemed to correspond with a genuine heart for God. His God-given gifts were massive; his intellect was titanic. He was one of the most influential leaders in the Church's history, and in fact remained to the present day a philosophical force to be reckoned with, even for secular scholars. Behind his intellectual influence, however, was a heart of almost total abandon to Jesus Christ. He became known as the *Doctor Gratia* (Doctor of Grace) because of his commitment to teach and contend for the gospel of grace against all compromises with legalism or human righteousness. This conviction had come from his study of Scripure, and was magnified by his own experience wrestling against temptations. He knew the human heart was so riddled with the infection called sin that only the sovereign, undeserved grace of God could save anyone. Throughout his believing years, he exerted his energies and gifts to proclaiming this gospel, the message which gives the greatest glory to Jesus Christ. Though certainly imperfect, he came closer to loving God with all his heart, soul, mind, and strength than any other of the individuals well known from earthly history books.

Then, Angela Moser of Hoboken was summoned, a woman of the late-nineteenth, early-twentieth centuries. At the mention of her name, I felt an entirely new kind of energy in the atmosphere; a sort of tingle or wave of excitement. Oddly, it did not seem to come from the assembled saints. From the human observers, there did not appear to be any unusual reaction.

"Uriel," I asked, "what just happened?"

"What you felt, I presume, is the rejoicing of the angelic hosts. Before you is Angela Moser, a saint so great that angels speak her name with awe."

"But who is she? I never heard of her before."

"Not many of your people have. She was largely unknown, even to many of her own neighbors during her lifetime. Her fame was wide among the angels, however."

"What did she do?" I asked.

"If you mean what great heroic action she accomplished, or what great organization she founded, she did neither. Her life was plain to those who judge according to appearance. She was a teacher of young children in public school. She cared for an elderly mother and invalid sister at home. She never married, though she greatly longed for a mate during her youth. She was a quiet and faithful member of her church. When she died, there were no headlines or state funeral.

"And yet I tell you, this woman was so great a warrior for our Lord that the enemy's agents trembled at her name. They feared her prayers more than a thousand angels. The heart of Angela Moser beat with the cadence of the Lord. If any fallen human ever loved God with an undivided heart, it was she. Her response to his urging was instantaneous. Her obedience to his Word was unquestioning. She knew his mind. When she prayed, it was from such intimacy with him that her entire humanity was a willing glove for his hand. Her inward eyes could see through the enemy's schemes from afar. She thwarted more evil than any human of whom I have ever known.

"Despite her godly hatred of sin and evil, she was a person of great love. Children's lives were never the same for having known her. She taught them, trained them, molded them—all in a rich blanket of love. She prayed for them, every one. Thousands, perhaps millions of lives were affected for the better, because this woman set life after life spinning away from her in concentric circles charged with the love and wisdom of God. Her quiet influence and her prayers influenced the lives of the many pastors who served her church. There was no sacrifice she would not make for love, and it was love of the right kind. Love born of truth, a well-adjusted and giving, rather than needy, love. She was so utterly filled up by the Lord Jesus that she needed little else.

"She of course had her own struggles. She earnestly desired a husband as a young woman, as I have said. The man she desired most, she decided, would have turned her heart away from God, and that was unacceptable. Then, too, her mother needed her care, then her sister, so she gave herself to what she believed was her God-given responsibility. While most people would have chafed in resentment and complaint over such a situation, she rejoiced. Every day was a day of rejoicing in her presence.

"Whether she was quietly ministering to others, teaching her children, or serving at her church, she followed the Scripture which says, 'pray without ceasing.' There were thousands of people whose lives were blessed in thousands of ways because God answered the prayers of Angela Moser of Hoboken. People were led to salvation; pastors ministered fruitfully; men earned honest provision for their families; women were blessed with husbands and children; criminals were reformed; the sick were healed. In fact, the greatest honor I was granted on earth was once to have been privileged to be God's messenger to answer one of her requests."

"But, Uriel," I asked, "don't all believers pray? Why were the prayers of this saint unusual? Surely the Lord doesn't play favorites."

"Not favorites as people on earth think of them," he answered. "He loves all, because he is love. Yet, all did not have the same intimacy of relationship with him. This is not because our Lord was reluctant, but because you people were. You desired God, and desired to keep him at arm's length at the same time. The rare person who was willing to open his or her heart to him, who trusted him with purity of motives, was the one that grew to know him best. In truth, any child of God could have been one of his favorites. For God was always looking for people of faith."

"Then why is it that people often complained that their prayers were not answered?"

"The greatest reason for unanswered prayers was unoffered prayers. Be assured of this: Your God was more willing to answer your requests than you were willing to make them. At heart, you all struggled with unbelief. You doubted that God is good, or that he loves you; or, you doubted that he has the wisdom to know the best and right thing to do; or, you doubted his power, that he has the ability to do what he wants to do in his goodness and wisdom. Think about it, Daniel Mathewson. If a person was unwilling to trust God in some area of life, the reason must have been at least one of those things. At heart, you did not really believe God wanted to answer your prayer, or that he was not able to do so.

"That is what made Angela Moser special, a woman after God's own heart. She had a complete trust in the love and goodness of God. She was willing to trust him with everything that ever happened to her, because she knew him to have all wisdom. And she carried a total confidence that the Lord had all authority and power to fulfill his promises. Therefore, she asked many things. She asked in accord with his character, because she knew him and his Word intimately, and she asked with assurance. One who knew God's nature and character so well, and who was totally surrendered to his will, would make requests often and was not likely to ask amiss."

The saint on the platform, Angela Moser, fell on her face before the Lord. She appeared completely devastated. The Lord Jesus walked to her, knelt and touched her, helping her to her feet. "Well done, Angela!" he said. "You are indeed a good and faithful servant!"

There was a blinding flash like a mighty lightning bolt, and she was transformed. A gasp of astonishment arose from the assembled saints as we looked upon a being of glory surpassing any we had seen, other than the Lord himself. Though we had seen the glorification of millions to this point, we had seen none like her. The degrees of glory to which believers can be lifted went far beyond my anticipation.

"This is my beloved Angela Moser," said the Lord Jesus, "in whom I am very well pleased." The overwhelmed and trembling multitude roared in their amazement and joy.

I thought of the biblical story of James and John asking to be seated at the Lord's right and left hand, meaning the places of highest honor and authority in the coming kingdom. Jesus turned down their request, saying that those places were reserved for the ones the Father would choose. I knew better than to believe I was competent to judge, but I was tempted to speculate that I had just seen a recipient of one of those seats.

CHAPTER 14

⁓

"**B**enjamin Ben Yosef of Kiev," cried the one whose name means, "Voice of God." This saint was one of those whom Uriel called the "kinsmen of the Lord"—an Israelite. This Russian Jew had lived in the eighteenth century, and had become a believer in Jesus as the Messiah through reading the New Testament in a Bible secretly given him by a friend. He identified himself with Christ at great personal cost. Benjamin was disowned by his family and community. His father conducted a funeral service for him and never spoke his name again. He had difficulty finding acceptance in the Christian community, as well. Despite openly professing his faith and devoting himself to diligent discipleship, he continued to be discriminated against because of his heritage. He experienced great difficulty even in finding honest employment, and therefore was wretchedly poor. Benjamin Ben Yosef lived out his days as a social leper to two worlds, unacceptable to any but God.

I had seen enough judgments by this time to begin to have a sense of proportion, a general idea of the nations and races represented in the Church. There were millions of Israelites from the first century, which was to be expected. After all, almost the whole first generation of Christians were Jews. And there were children of Israel dotting the history of the Church throughout the centuries. I found it disheartening, however, to learn how few of Abraham's children had received by faith the "promised seed," the Savior, through whom the whole world would be blessed. After the initial flood in the first century, the influx of Jewish Christians dwindled to a bare trickle. Though there was again a surge of conversions in the twentieth century, still the remnant of Israel was tiny in comparison to many of the nations found in the Church.

For this—to speak truly—Christians were as responsible as anyone. It would be hard to conceive of a more effective campaign to hinder people from coming to Jesus Christ than that waged against the Jewish people by professing Christians over twenty centuries. I have spoken of the wonder and joy I experienced as I watched the judgments, but there is another side to the story. As we learned of the individual lives of wonderful believers through the centuries, we learned of many terrible things, too.

For a long time, Christians were a persecuted minority in the Roman Empire. After the conversion of Emperor Constantine and the legalization of Christianity, however, the church quickly grew in political power. Before long, the organized church was *the* power in the western world, looming above emperors and kings. Human sin always congregates wherever you find the unholy trinity of power, money, and sex, and by the Middle Ages, the "church" held the greatest concentration of power in the world. The well-known statement is true: "Power tends to corrupt, and absolute power corrupts absolutely." The brew of power, wealth, and the usual perks that go with them was far too intoxicating for fallen human beings to resist, so the "church" became a den of iniquity the likes of which the world has seldom seen.

It was a "church" like this that persecuted, tortured, and starved the kinsmen of our Lord. The Jews were driven from place to place. They were barred from most occupations. They were forced to live in ghettos. They were periodically attacked without warning. They were commanded to "convert" to Christ on the threat of torture and death. They were blamed for the Black Plague and were persecuted. They were blamed for Muslims conquering the Holy Land and were persecuted. They were blamed for natural disasters, famines, and losses in war and were persecuted. Even over the age of Reformation, when the Word of God and the gospel of God's grace were returned to the people, there lies this black stain: further slander and opposition to the Jews by both Protestants and Catholics.

God must have preserved the children of Israel through the years, or they surely would have perished. It seems as if all the nations of the world conspired together to destroy the Jews.

Every people and country took their turn in this history of hatred. Roman centurions drove them from their homes. Medieval bishops incited bloodthirsty mobs to burn them out. Crusading knights with crosses on their garments and shields killed them in the name of Christ. Russian colonels carried out the *pogroms* (officially sanctioned persecutions). Great Britain betrayed and abandoned them in the twentieth century after having promised them a homeland in Palestine. Finally, Hitler's henchmen did their worst in the concentration camps.

Horribly, all these represented Jesus Christ to the persecuted people. We could protest that no one who truly knew Christ would do such things, but it would ring hollow. Even if true, how could we expect *them* to discern the difference between genuine and merely professing Christians? It all happened in "Christendom." The centurion was serving a "Christian" empire. The bishop was himself an official of the "church." The knight was a "Servant of the Cross." The Russian nation was at least nominally Orthodox Christian for many centuries. England was a "Christian nation." Germany *claimed* allegiance to Lutheran Christianity. Sadistic Nazis taunted doomed Jews on their way to the gas ovens beneath the sign of the swastika, itself a *twisted cross*. Many genuine Christians throughout history *did* behave terribly. The treatment of the Jews for twenty centuries by falsely professing "Christians" *and by genuine believers* was inexcusable.

After learning of these things, I was no longer surprised that so few of the Lord's kinsmen had come to faith in him. It now seemed miraculous that any of them had.

My evident wrestling with this issue shows that all mysteries were not explained at the Bema. One I remain puzzled about is this: How God will judge people for their unbelief whose only exposure to Christianity was of a degraded, twisted, or hypocritical type. More than ever before, I know God's love, mercy, and justice, and I am sure whatever God does will be consistent and in harmony with those attributes. But still I remain in the dark on this issue.

Like Ezekiel the prophet, I can only bow my head in humility and say, "Lord, you know."

I gave thanks that there was always a believing, if small, remnant of Israel in the Church, which in turn raised another question in my mind. "Uriel," I said, "all of the Jewish people I have seen at the Bema were Christians after the Lord's coming. What of all the others? What of Abraham, Moses, and Daniel? Of all the millions who were surely faithful in Old Testament times?"

"They are not here, for they are not of the Church," he replied. "The Church consists of those believers in this unique period between Pentecost and the Lord's coming for you. The assembly in which there is no Jew or Gentile, but all are one in Christ Jesus."

I was puzzled. "But what will happen to the others? Will they not be judged?"

"Certainly," answered the angel. "All who ever walked on the earth will be judged, but each at the proper time and place. People often spoke of 'Judgment Day,' but they were indistinct. There are many judgment days. The Church has her own, in which you are participating. Israel of the Old Covenant will have her own, too. Believing Israelites who lived before our Lord's death and resurrection will be raised to life again to join in the kingdom when it is restored to earth. Such was promised in the prophets, and it was their fervent hope. Do you not remember the Lord's words regarding John the Baptist? He said, 'Among them that are born of women there has not risen any greater than John the Baptist: nevertheless, he that is least in the kingdom of heaven is greater than he.' He did not mean greatness of heart, faith, or courage. He meant greatness of status, of position. The lowliest member of this assembly you see possesses a position of honor to which men and angels will bow in the kingdom. John himself recognized this, which is why he referred to himself as the friend of the Bridegroom. He knew he was not of the bride. To be in the Church—a member of Christ's body, his bride—is a privilege beyond description.

"There will be others as well. Many more Gentiles of the Old Testament period became believers in the Lord than you have ever heard. While there were many dark years in Israel's history, there were also many times when their witness was bright. Times in which they were a shining lamp in a dark world of paganism, and they drew many to the knowledge of the true God. A few of their names you know from your Bible: Naaman the leper, a Syrian; Ruth the Moabitess; Nebuchadnezzar the king of Babylon. Some after believing took on the yoke of the Law and entered the house of Israel. Some entered the tent of Israel by marriage, such as Ruth or Rahab of Jericho. Millions more became believers in Israel's God without becoming members of Israel. They will also receive a heavenly inheritance after experiencing their own judgment."

I thought of my early observations upon entering the heavenlies, that God likes variety and distinctions. It seems I was right, and there was much more to learn.

"And then there will be those believers of Israel who die on earth during the tribulation period, and the multitude of Gentiles who will be saved …"

"Wait!" I interrupted Uriel. My attention was captured by another saint on the platform. I had not noticed anything unusual when a person named Joseph Ray Robinson was called. His biographical sketch was positive but unremarkable. Born in the midwestern United States during the Depression and raised by a godly mother, he had memorized hundreds of Bible verses before the age of ten. He grew up to be an honest, hard-working family man. He would take on any honorable work to feed and clothe his eight children, as well as to share with needy people in his neighborhood. He delivered papers, he shined shoes, he worked as a conductor on passenger trains, he drove limousines, he worked in an office building...

It was Joe Thesecurityguard!

After bolting upright in my seat and interrupting Uriel, I riveted my attention on the platform. A wonderful saintly life was shown to us by Kolael. Few saints could surpass Joseph Robinson's knowledge of Jesus Christ or love for the Word of God. Joseph enjoyed an intimate relationship with the Savior, and his life became a conduit through which Christ touched thousands of others. With mature, yet childlike, faith, he walked confidently through a life full of trials, discrimination, and injustice. He had been denied higher education as a young man because of his race, a terrible shame for one so intellectually gifted. He was denied chances for achievement or promotions that were well within his capabilities dozens of times. Yet, he never gave in to bitterness or hatred. He entrusted himself to the Lord Jesus, and continued to love and serve people. He was ready at any moment to explain the good news, and personally led hundreds of people to faith in Christ. He counseled the distressed and encouraged the downcast. He sincerely prayed for others who were above him in social status and far below him in spiritual substance. Without being told, I knew I was in that company.

Joseph's judgment completed, the Lord addressed the assembly. "This is my beloved Joseph Robinson, in whom I am well pleased." The saint burned with surpassing glory. Would I be worthy to shine *his* shoes in the kingdom age? I wondered.

A million or so judgments later, another saint was summoned in whom I had a personal interest.

"Juanita Perez De Cuellar," called the herald. After receiving only a portion of her sketch, I knew that this was the cleaning woman at my office. Again, I was amazed at the spiritual depth and character of someone I had thought hardly worthy of notice on earth.

Juanita was the daughter of immigrants, having moved to the United States at age nine. She struggled to learn English (her parents never did learn), and thus had great trouble in school. She dropped out after the seventh grade and went to work cleaning homes with her mother. At seventeen, Juanita married Carlos Perez and soon gave birth to a boy. Two more boys and a girl followed in the next ten years. With children of her own beginning to attend school, Juanita realized her need to learn in order to help them. Hearing of a conversational English and literacy class at a small church nearby, she enrolled. This mission church used those classes as an opportunity for community service, and also as an evangelistic outreach. They used the English Bible as one of their tools to teach the language, and it was in this way that Juanita first heard the gospel. She received Jesus as her Savior, and later led her husband and each of her children to faith in Christ.

With new impetus for living, Juanita worked hard to learn English and make up for her lost education. She eventually earned a high school equivalency diploma and went on to become proficient in word processing—her preparation for working in the law office that she mentioned to me. After fifteen years of marriage, Carlos was struck in the head and killed by a girder that came loose while working at a construction site. Juanita applied her strong faith to carrying on, providing for herself and her children. She worked double shifts, sometimes three part-time jobs at once. Even with such handicaps on her time, Juanita's influence and teaching was strong enough to shape and mold those children. In spite of the many long hours she spent away from them, they all grew to be mature, dedicated Christians. She was able to send each of her three sons to college, and was about to enroll her daughter when the Lord came for us.

Most of all, her love and godliness stood out to those who knew her. She was never known to sink into self-pity, despite the many challenges she faced. She was happy, positive, and encouraging to others. Many sought her out for motherly advice. Many more sought her to intercede for them in prayer. Working hard nighttime hours cleaning office buildings, she spent the time singing and praying. Never jealous, she prayed for the prosperity and blessing of others. And always, she gave thanks to the Lord who loved her, who had saved her, and who always provided for her.

Once again, I was humbled. Crossing her path so often in the mornings before work, I had always treated her with cool reserve, never realizing the privilege I had been granted just to be in the presence of so great a saint.

Several millions more took their turn on the platform. Looking around the great stadium, I estimated that about two-thirds of those present had been evaluated. Now, back in their seats and shining in various degrees of glory, the stands of the arena looked like a great circular galaxy of brilliant stars. It was a breathtakingly beautiful sight.

As he had done tens of millions of times before, Kolael the herald faced the assembly and struck the butt end of staff. Somehow, I felt I knew whom he would call next. "Daniel Scott Mathewson," he cried.

CHAPTER 15

It did not occur to me at the time to wonder how I knew it was me the angel summoned. After all, there were many Daniel Scott Mathewsons present, as there were many of other personal names. Some kind of individual call was clearly involved that each one perceived intuitively. I knew for certain it was for me Kolael looked.

I was too overwhelmed for conscious thought as I was flown by angelic power to the floor of the arena. I did not know if it was Uriel who carried me (I found out later he did not). I could only fix my eyes on the platform growing nearer, and, most of all, on the One seated on the Bema.

My feet planted on the floor, I looked up the steps before me. Kolael stood at the top right, rigid as a sentry with his blazing eyes staring me through. God must have been strengthening me as I began to climb the stair, because I don't believe I would otherwise have had the power even to stand. I felt that combination of emotions I had felt before when anticipating this event: quivering fear in every fiber of my body, but reinforced with complete confidence in the goodness, kindness, and justice of the Lord. I climbed the steps deliberately, as if to file each one in my memory. Half way to the top, I could see the Lord on his throne. If I had found his appearance overwhelming from afar, his beauty and power up close surpassed my earlier impressions beyond the capacity of words. Directly above him, hovering behind the Bema, was the manifest presence of God the Father. Seeing them both in one visual perspective made everything else disappear from notice, almost as if they drew into themselves the whole universe. Even the otherwise impressive Kolael, just a few feet from me, seemed to fade away. I still had no conscious thoughts. I felt only that thoughtless, wordless experience men call awe.

I reached the top of the platform and stood, waiting. How can I describe what it meant to look into the face of my Savior? How can I describe with a feeble earth vocabulary what he looked like? To describe that Face, I could use words an earthly reader can understand, such as nobility, kindness, wisdom, and authority. And they would be true descriptions, so long as the reader would know not to limit them to those qualities seen in worldly counterparts. For in him, those qualities are found in essence. He is the source, the archetype, of all of them.

Most of all, in that Face I saw love. And in spite of the holy fear I felt, I loved him in return. I felt that I was looking at the One I had always longed to see, even when I did not know what I was longing for. All those elusive emotions I described before—such as the ache for Paradise I felt while watching the sun rise, or the fanfare of the heavenly trumpet that seemed a sound from my real home—

were just precursors of this moment. To be united with him was the purpose of existence. To be reunited with him was the purpose of redemption. I felt I understood what some of the old Christian writers meant when they referred to the "Beatific Vision"—that to see the face of God would itself be Heaven. In truth, I believe I could have stood at that spot forever gazing at him and been completely fulfilled and happy.

With a kind smile on his face and gentleness in his voice, he spoke: "Welcome, Daniel. Approach the throne."

Feeling stronger and inwardly ready for whatever the Lord willed to do, I walked to a spot about ten feet from him and stopped.

"Daniel," he said, "it is time for you to give an account of your stewardship. A stewardship is a trust. Since every man and woman has been granted a unique quantity and combination of stewardships, all must be evaluated individually according to what has been given each one. Do you understand?"

"Yes, Lord," I answered.

"You have been given life in the time and place my Father chose for you, that you might carry out his will. You were given thirty-seven years of life on earth, of which twenty-five years were after your conversion. You were called to salvation, justified, and recreated in me for good works, which my Father prepared beforehand that you might walk in them and glorify him. You were also given spiritual gifts with which to serve joyfully and fruitfully in the power of the Holy Spirit.

"In addition to these things, there are the specific stewardships that were entrusted to you, such things as your family relationships, including a wife and children. There were of course relationships, or potential relationships, with many other people. People you could love, serve, and influence. You were given a measure of wealth to use, and a measure of health to serve. You have been given opportunities on a daily basis for which you would choose faith or unbelief, love or pride, to serve others or seek to be served yourself.

"There are two important reasons for this judgment to be conducted at this time. First, because only now, at the end of the age, is it possible for the true results of people's actions to be evident. Human decisions affect many others besides the individual in question. Others are affected, and, because they are changed, many others are affected. Human lives on earth are a vast web. The plucking of a single strand sends out vibrations and ripples far and wide. Sometimes, centuries are required to complete the harvest of spiritual fruit, or the harvest of dire consequences, of individuals' lives and choices. Thus, the decision of rewards or lack thereof must have waited until now. Do you understand this?"

"I think so, Lord," I replied, trying to take it all in.

"The second reason for the judgment to take place at this time is for the sake of truth. You have lived your life in a world of illusions, partial truths, and deceptions. Besides these, self-deception is a chief consequence of sin. No one self-deceived is prepared for life in the heavenlies. I will soon establish my kingdom on earth, and all my servants will assume their proper places of service in my administration. No man or woman who carries illusions about himself is prepared for that role. My eyes search the hearts of men, and nothing is hidden from my sight. Now, you must come to know yourself just as you are known by me."

Had I not been strengthened by the grace of the Lord, I surely would have collapsed on the spot from the alarm in my soul. Of all things, I believe I most feared confronting the real truth about myself. In a moment of sudden realization, I knew how much of my life I had spent and how much effort I had expended living as a fugitive from the truth. But right here, all my evasions, excuses, and rationalizations were about to be stripped away forever. I was standing before him who is the Truth, and he was going to direct the blinding light of his eyes into every nook and cranny of my soul. The flame of truth was going to test the quality of my life and works, even my thoughts and motives. The real worth of my character and life was going to be manifested for all the universe to see.

And yet, as strange as it may seem, I felt after the initial surge of fear an immediate second reaction of great relief. What a relief it will be to lay down the burden of pretense! Finally to come out of the shadows into the bright light of the Lord's day, to be set free by the truth. The encouragement of a Bible verse I had memorized long ago came to mind: "There is no fear in love. But perfect love drives out fear, because fear has to do with punishment. The one who fears is not made perfect in love." The purpose of this judgment was not punishment. It was to reveal what was eternally worthy. In recalling that verse, I remembered also another phrase in the same context that had always seemed impossible: "In this way, love is made complete among us so that we will have confidence on the day of judgment..." Confidence on the day of judgment!? How could that be? I always wondered. Now I understood. The One who is the

Truth is also Love, and his perfect love had driven away my fear.

The Lord continued. "I will put your life to the test. You will see your life as I have seen it. You will be able to listen to your thoughts, observe your actions, and see the consequences. You will see yourself through my eyes, and also through the eyes of other people. Those parts of your life and service that are worthy of reward shall endure the judgment. All else shall be burned away forever.

"The first years of your life were lived alienated from me. After your twelfth year, you were capable of spiritual service, and therefore of earning rewards. You will observe from your childhood, nevertheless, because it shows from where you began, and the foundation of personality, training, and experience you had to build on. Simple production is not the criterion of the judgment. I will take into account what each person had to work with in evaluating his faithfulness."

He paused for a moment, then said, "You may ask me questions whenever you wish. Let us begin."

I had heard many stories of people having near-death experiences and reporting that they saw their whole life flash before their eyes. I don't know if those reports were genuine, but at the Bema I experienced the real thing.

In one sense, the judgment was almost instantaneous. Assuming that my evaluation was like all the others I had seen, it only took a minute or two according to the perceptions of the observers. On the other hand, it seemed like years, almost as if it took longer to observe my thirty-seven years than it did to actually live them. Time in the heavenlies continued to prove elastic. While time on earth proceeded normally according to people's perceptions, there was a different measure of time in the heavenlies, another at the Bema, and a separate pace for each individual at the moment of judgment. Eternity was proving to be much more than just time infinitely extended. Only the Lord knows how many spheres within spheres of time were operating within his creation.

It is difficult to describe the process of judgment. It could best be communicated by a few analogies, none of which is perfect.

Looked at as an instantaneous event, it would be like this: Imagine your whole life and works as a house built of various materials: some valuable, like gold and silver; some cheap, like wood and thatch; some trash. A massive flame-thrower blasts it. All that is flammable goes up in smoke, leaving only ashes that blow away in the wind. The precious metals remain. Actually, they more than remain. They are *purified*. Any impurities in them are burned out, leaving only pure gold and silver.

Viewed as a more gradual process, imagine an ornate tapestry. It is woven of valuable gold and silver thread, and cheap and worthless thread. Its designs tell a detailed story of a life, a life of mixed quality. It is part dull and earthy, part positively evil. But it also contains some beautiful scenes of God's handiwork. A fire is kindled at one edge, which begins to burn across the tapestry. The cheap threads that make up the ugly scenes are burned to ashes as the fire reaches them. The beautiful scenes woven of gold and silver, however, shine even brighter as all that is unworthy around them falls away. At the end of the fire, only those beautiful things made of the precious material remain.

Looked at as a long process, it seemed to me that I took a walk through my life as the Lord's eyes burned away every unworthy thing in the story. I simply watched and listened as my life unfolded. He did not speak except in answer to my questions, which were few. I passed through most incidents in my life quickly, because viewed in the light of the Lord's truth it was obvious what was there to see and learn. Usually, I merely nodded and said quietly, "Yes, Lord. I see," and we moved on. Sometimes, though, I lingered over an incident in my life, either struck by entirely new insight into something I misunderstood on earth, or because I wanted the Lord to help me understand what had happened.

I began to gain self-understanding from the first instant. I saw my birth (an amazing experience in itself!), and saw my infant self being cared for by my parents. Immediately, knowing how I later came to think and act as an adult, I was convicted of my life-long arrogance. If challenged on earth, I would have professed to be free of prejudice, snobbery, or bigotry. In my heart, though, I went through life with an attitude of superiority that, even viewed on a natural level, was nonsensical. In the searchlight of the Lord's eyes, I saw what I never consciously realized before: I was actually proud of who and what I was, as if I had something to do with it! These are difficult things to write, for they will surely cause a reader to wonder about my mental state, but this is what I learned: I felt superior to other people because I was born of my particular class in twentieth-century America. Somehow, slightly and half-consciously, I looked down on others who were not.

My attitude said: "Well, after all, those minorities and those people who live in poor places like India are only getting what they deserve. If they had been on the ball like me, they would have gotten themselves born in America in the twentieth century to upper-middle-class white parents. It's their own fault."

Who did I think I was, to have such an attitude? Once you look directly at it, could there be a more idiotic state of mind than bigotry and racism? More than idiotic, they are really slanders of God, who made people what they are, and placed them where and when he pleased. If anyone had brought a remnant of snobbery, bigotry, or racism to the heavenlies, it was surely completely and forever pulverized after the Bema judgments.

Seeing my young parents doing their best to care for me, I noticed other things of which I had no memory. For example, I did not remember the spare, dingy apartment we lived in before I turned three. Most of my recollections of growing up centered on the nice suburban neighborhoods we lived in later. I never realized from what humble beginnings my family arose, nor how hard my father worked to give us a better lifestyle. I took it all for granted, as if it were a birthright. To be painfully honest, my parents in those early years were just the kind of people I looked down on later in life.

How ugly! Still, my education was only beginning.

CHAPTER 16

🙠

It was a wonderful mercy that the purpose of this judgment was not to expose and punish sins, for they seemed omnipresent in my life. The Lord Jesus continually sustained me with the knowledge of his forgiveness and of my justification in him. He never condemned me (in fact, I'm not at all sure that he even "saw" my sins—at least not as I "saw" them), but it still grieved me to watch myself do evil. Now having a heavenly perspective, it astonished me to see the brazen way I chose to commit sin. Though I never lost the clear knowledge that I was observing myself, in another sense I frequently felt I was watching the antics of some insane beast.

Beyond actions, though, it was positively mind-numbing to hear my thoughts. How could an intelligent being be so foolish? So wicked? So completely absorbed in oneself? My selfishness was horrifying. My self-pity was sickening. What a sad, ugly tragedy to have been given the gift of life on earth, and to have spent so much of it in a mental state like this! And it was not only as a grownup. While I grew more sophisticated in how I expressed indwelling sin, the rotten root was in my nature from birth. I saw the same character in myself as a two year-old that I could see in mature form as an adult. I was like most two year-olds: willing to throw a temper tantrum, hold my breath until I turned blue, beat my head on the floor—whatever it took to get my own way. As an adult, I was just as determined to get my own way. I merely became more clever and sophisticated in how I went about it. A Bible verse came to mind that said in part, "the hearts of men, moreover, are full of evil and there is madness in their hearts while they live." "Yes, Lord," I said, "it was true in my case. I was spiritually insane with the madness called sin." For the first time I really believed the words of the apostle Paul: "nothing good lives in me, that is, in my flesh."

What a joy to watch the moment of my conversion! To watch that sad twelve year-old boy wrestle with his sense of identity, with guilt, and with fear of God's penal judgment, and find peace through believing the good news. Whatever paths I wandered later and however I might have stumbled, I never lost the clear certainty that I was one of his, that I was a child of God by faith in Jesus Christ. "Thank you, Lord Jesus," I said. "Thank you for dying to become my Savior. Thank you for that faithful pastor who proclaimed your gospel, and thank you for Mrs. Foncannon, that faithful Sunday School teacher who talked to me, and told me how I could accept your free gift and have you come and live in my heart."

Watching this crucial event in my life, I glanced at the Lord Jesus. He seemed to have tears in his eyes, and his face was full of emotion. I felt too shy and humble to speak, but words were unnecessary. I knew it in my soul. He was experiencing the same compassionate, merciful love that had motivated him to become a man, go to a cross, and die on my behalf. He loved me! I was overwhelmed with the knowledge.

It would be nice to say that, from the day of my conversion, my sinning was over and I lived for God every moment of every day. But of course that would not even be close to the truth. Christ did indeed live in me, but so did sin. And I continued to wrestle with sin in the following years.

But along with the observing of my sins came also the most wonderful of truths. Even as I saw the sin, I knew that it was burned away by the eyes of the Lord as part of the wood, hay, and stubble—the worthless things of my life. The guilt was not mine to bear. For in the great exchange of the cross, my guilt had been transferred to his account and his righteousness had been credited to mine. His shed blood had taken away my guilt once and for all, and I stood before him fully justified, as righteous as he. The purpose for seeing my sins at all at the Bema was that I might have true self-knowledge, not for condemnation. And true self-knowledge is indeed what I was receiving.

Since the day I became a Christian, and for years afterward, I felt genuine relief and gratitude for the forgiveness of my sins. But I was beginning to learn that forgiveness for my *sins* was not my only need. My problem was far deeper than that. To get to the heart of the matter, I needed salvation from *what I was*, not just from what I had *done*. I thought I understood the meaning of grace before this, but I had barely scratched the surface. I knew the biblical teaching that "all have sinned and fall short of the glory of God," but my understanding went little deeper than the acknowledgment that "nobody's perfect." In the presence of the righteous Lord, it was appalling to listen to a mind laced with the madness of sin. On my best day, I was still on my own merits light years short of the standard of righteousness acceptable to God. Never again would I have the slightest doubt but that I had been saved by sheer grace.

I do not mean to give the impression that the judgment was all about seeing sin. There were many good things to see, too, but it should be understandable that the strongest first impressions were these. Now in the heavenlies, in the presence of the Holy One, in a remade body without indwelling sin, I was seeing my fallen self really for the first time. It was like having always thought that you were a taller-than-average person, and then finding yourself in a land of giants whose toes you cannot see over. My earthly conception of goodness and holiness were so limited and watered down that I had thought myself a pretty good person. What the Lord said about our living in a world of illusions and self-deceptions was absolutely right. It was an overwhelming experience to begin to see the truth.

I learned so much about myself from the judgment that I must drastically edit what I relate. Rather than follow a strict chronological order of my life's progress, I will share some observations according to a few different categories and perspectives.

I gained clear eyesight about more than right and wrong. As I watched myself develop through childhood and adolescence to adulthood, I could see the big picture of how I became the person I did. I was used to learning the personalities and habits of others. With people I knew well, I frequently got to a point where I could predict their attitudes, actions, and reactions with a fair degree of accuracy. But the person I never saw from outside was myself. At the Bema, I learned from an outsider's viewpoint what made me tick, and it surprised me in many ways.

Patterns began to emerge very early. In childhood I had a strong desire to be liked, and hated to be left out of what the other kids were doing. That quality was normal and neutral in itself, but like all natural things, could be turned toward evil where God was not in the picture.

I saw a scene of myself at age eleven at a playground with a group of friends. Among them was my best friend, a red-haired, freckle-faced boy named Jimmy. (One of the great delights of the Bema judgment was this, to see again people and events that were only vague memories years later).

Jimmy and I were inseparable. On this occasion, we were playing on the monkey bars and slides of the park, just enjoying a fun summer day. A group of ten or twelve other boys came over to us, and asked me to play baseball with them. These boys were not particularly bad, but they were not my usual playmates. They were, in fact, the cool kids, the *in* group at school. To be honest, I very much wished to be a part of that circle, but never could break in. "We need one more," they said, looking directly at me.

"What about Jimmy?" I asked.

"We just need one more player," they repeated.

I really wanted to play with them. The few seconds of silence seemed like minutes. I looked down at the ground, then took a slight sideways glance at Jimmy. "Go ahead if you want," Jimmy said. "I don't care."

"Are you sure?" I asked hopefully.

Jimmy shrugged. "I don't want to play. I need to do something at home." He jumped off the monkey bars and walked away. I played baseball that afternoon.

It was terrible to watch. I knew Jimmy was hurt. Out of the corner of my eye, I could see his ears and face blush red, accentuated by his fair, freckled complexion. I heard the slight tremble in his voice. But I chose to ignore what I knew to be true, and did what I wanted to do, what was in my best interest. My desire to be *in* was so strong that I was willing to hurt my best friend.

Eleven year-olds do that kind of thing, I know. It was an incident that took only a few moments of time. And yet, characters are built brick-by-brick through the accumulation of such moments. This proved to be a very telling scene in my development.

A few years passed, and I was in that difficult stage called early adolescence. My hunger for acceptance by the in-crowd only deepened. Every era, at least in our western culture, had its own correct hairstyles and clothing. Usually, it is the cool set that determines locally what those will be, who is in and who is out. I was out, and the maddening thing at the time was that I could never figure out why. When you are fourteen, you don't have the maturity or perspective to see how arbitrary that behavior is or how stupid it will look years later. You only know how much it hurts.

It was painful now to watch my desperate efforts to gain acceptance. "What's wrong with me?" I would ask. "Your hair is all wrong," some "helpful friend" would say. And so I fought the "Hair Wars" with my father, a 1950s holdout. We had vicious emotional conflicts, which Dad never understood, over how long I could grow my hair. To him it was all completely absurd, but to me it was a life and death struggle for acceptance. I won, mainly through wearing him down. But I was not accepted by the in-crowd.

"What else is wrong?" I asked. "Your clothes aren't cool," they said, and so I fought the "Clothes Wars" (and let's not even comment on the fashions of the 1970s!). I eventually got my cool clothes, but I still wasn't accepted.

"What else is wrong?" I asked. "You dance like a dork," they said. Let's not go into my efforts to learn cool dancing in the 70s, either.

All told, over two or three years, I did everything in my power to understand and do whatever it took to be accepted by the cool set, and never accomplished it.

These are just two examples of what was clearly a life-long tendency. I asked, "Lord, this is so sad. Why were the opinions of other people so important? Was my sense of self that weak?"

"This is always the way," he answered, "when people do not come to me as the bread of life. There is a drive in every human being for love and acceptance, for meaning and purpose in life, and for a sense of identity. Only I can satisfy those needs. If one does not come to me, he must try to fill that vacuum with things of the world: with people, places, and things—none of which can satisfy the human heart. Many of the foolish and evil things people do are motivated by these inner hungers."

It was certainly true in my case. Much of the behavior in my life grew out of my desire to be *in*. I drank my first beer (though I didn't like the taste) to be part of the group. I tried smoking marijuana (though I *really* didn't like how it made my lungs feel) because I was afraid of the group's disapproval. I joined a fraternity in college (though I knew it was mainly an organization to promote partying, and didn't square with my Christian commitment) because I wanted to be part of a group. I wanted to walk around campus with those Greek letters on my shirt, because those "Independents," as we called them, were considered nobodies. There must have been something wrong with them, or they would have been in a fraternity. Nobody wanted them (we thought).

In my first year at college, I developed a friendship with a guy named Jerry. We used to run around together, along with three other fellows from our dormitory floor. We didn't care (much) that we weren't among the in-crowd of the Freshman class. We were too shy to date, so we mainly enjoyed sports. Here was one area in which I was above average. I played quarterback for our intramural touch- football team, and was the second leading scorer on our basketball team. Jerry wasn't much of an athlete, but he was always fun to have around.

Then came fraternity rush. Fraternities and sororities at our college had a sharp and well known social pecking order. For example, everyone knew which three fraternities were at the top. Then came the second level of fraternities, which were socially acceptable, but not top drawer. Then at the bottom were three or four groups that were considered nerds (even by themselves, amazingly!). In social interaction, the fraternities and sororities kept strictly to those strata. A top-level sorority, for example, would never hold a joint party with a fraternity below the top three. Likewise, mid-level sororities interacted at or above their level, but never below.

It was a terrible system, but not unusual in the world. In fact, I believe this system only brought into plain view the same human values that could be seen on any playground or corporate office. From the viewpoint of the heavenlies, though, it was simply an expression of ugly human arrogance and pride.

My friends and I sized up our probabilities for acceptance during rush. We figured that we were likely to be counted above the level of nerds, but definitely not in the top level. We decided that, whatever happened, we would stick together and join the same fraternity.

My commitment lasted until I received a bid from one of the top three. I was blown away. After so many years of trying to get into the in-crowd, here I was being surprised by an offer of acceptance. Socially, I knew I didn't belong there. The only way it made sense was athletically. They wanted me for their intramural teams.

I was so flattered by their attention that my head was floating above the clouds. Attending a party with one of the top sororities, I could hardly express intelligent thoughts. Needless to say, I pledged that fraternity without a second thought about my commitment to my friends.

Jerry and I seldom saw each other after that, as I entered a whirlwind of social activity. It is horrible to admit, but at the Bema it was undeniable: Now that I was *in*, Jerry and the others were *below* me. God forgive me.

These are just a few examples of my pursuit. Of how I spent huge amounts of time and energy jumping through hoops for other people. Always seeking to be accepted, always wanting to become Somebody, but not caring who else I hurt as I climbed.

A pattern was emerging, one that would shed enormous light on the direction my life took years later.

CHAPTER 17

❧

One undeniable lesson of the Bema was value the Lord places on people. He loves people and values them far beyond my previous conception. In fact, much of his evaluation of the saints centered on how they affected other people, for good or ill.

I watched my life unfold, and it was sadly evident that I did not share much of the Lord's attitude. I thought of people as merely the scenery of my life. They were the backdrop, the playing field, often the competition. They were just there, at best. They were tools and instruments to be used, at worst.

This is not to say that I didn't love anyone. I possessed all the loves that are natural to man: I loved my parents, brother and sister; I loved my wife and children; I loved my friends. But I was so self-centered in my thoughts, motives, and desires, that the love of which I was capable was shallow to the extreme. Far more than I was aware, my love depended on such things as circumstances, comfort, and simply getting my own way. It was extremely flimsy and defenseless if it conflicted with something else I wanted. Apart from a heart of character that has learned to see as God sees and hold his values, human love is too weak to withstand much of a challenge.

Therefore, seeing the people in my life was the chief joy of the Bema, and at the same time the hardest truth to observe. Much of the joy came simply from seeing them again. Viewing my life as a whole, it was astonishing how brief was the time my life intersected with others'. People seemed to zip on and off the stage like vehicles flashing by on a freeway. I knew the Bible taught the brevity of life, and I had frequently heard older people speak of how short life was, but it had never sunk in. Now I understood. More wonderful people crossed paths with me during my lifetime than I could count, but I hardly noticed them at the time. I missed multitudes of opportunities to be enriched by others, and I missed as many opportunities to be a positive influence in others' lives.

I also learned how much others had served me, often totally without my awareness. I was oblivious as I grew up to how much I had been loved and served by my mother and father, or how much they sacrificed their own interests and desires for me. I was also unaware until now of how ungrateful I had been. I did not know how much grief and pain I caused them through my adolescent rebellion and nastiness.

As the stream of my life continued to flow by, some very good things began to be revealed. At a difficult and critical period of my life (junior year, age 16), I was invited by a school friend to a Sunday night youth activity at his church. I did not have much interest, but went anyway for some reason. To my surprise, I enjoyed it very much. The other kids seemed normal, accepted each other—and me—and seemed to be having fun. I also felt that the youth pastor, Randall Burton, took a particular interest in me. Now watching these things, I saw that he did indeed go the extra mile for me. My attitudes and behavior were not very appealing, but he looked past them to see my emptiness and need. Jesus Christ was reaching out to touch me through this man. "Burt," as we all called him, seemed an unlikely candidate to lead an influential youth ministry, but he did it wonderfully for many years. When I met him he was about fifty, but we teenagers felt completely comfortable with him. Always smiling and approachable, he actually seemed to like us.

In just a few weeks, I was a fixture at the group, enthusiastically participating in every activity. Watching now from the Bema, my youthful seriousness was amusing, though in an attractive way. I took so seriously the discussions we had on such things as the meaning of life. When we took on a service activity, I did it with all my might. Best of all, through Burt's influence I became an enthusiastic Bible student. I read the New Testament all the way through twice before the beginning of my senior year, and I regularly peppered Burt with theological problems and questions. I began to grow as a Christian for the first time.

It was heartwarming to see such energy and honest enthusiasm directed toward spiritual things. Certainly, there was also much of the awkwardness and rough edges of youth, but how refreshing to see it in comparison to the cynicism and complacency I later developed. I was truly happy then. God was very real to me, and Jesus Christ seemed my constant companion. The social pressures at school grew less important as my focus became more locked in on the Lord and doing his will.

Burt made me leader of a "faith group," a small cell group within the whole. I became a "pastor" of a group of eighteen other young people. It was a turning point in my life. It was the first time I had ever been granted a position of leadership, and as humble as the sphere might have been, it showed me that I had potential. The other kids looked up to me and were willing to follow. At the time, though, the most important thing to me was serving the Lord. I gave it all I had with all diligence. I made calls to the other kids, trying to make sure that everyone felt included. I knew what it was like to feel rejected, so I tried to make our group meetings fun and accepting for all. I tried to set an atmosphere where anyone could feel welcome, and forcefully did my best to eliminate the slightest hint of snobbery or judgmental attitudes.

A light clicked on in my understanding. I said, "Lord, I felt such pain when I was rejected or left out of things. I see now that it led me to do many things I shouldn't have. But here it seems that it helped me to do some good things. Is that right?"

"Yes, Daniel," he answered. "Life on earth contains many kinds of pain and suffering, but I have promised to cause all things to work together for good for those who belong to me. I, too, know what it is like to be rejected. Your hatred of being left out and your knowledge of the hurt that results gave you understanding of others' feelings. If you attended to that knowledge and were motivated by compassion, you were able to help others deal with the same. Your hurts helped prepare you to be a more effective servant for me."

Yes, I thought. Suffering is still suffering and pain still hurts, even if you are a Christian. But the Lord is infinitely creative and cannot be defeated. He can take anything, even that which is evil, and use it as raw materials to produce a greater good.

I saw again a freshman girl in that group, named Sandy. I don't know why I took a particular interest in her, but I saw her quietly sitting on the fringes and tried to draw her in. She was painfully shy and seldom said a word, even when directly asked, but she kept coming regularly. I made a point of talking to her at youth gatherings, and tried to make her feel a part of the group. On some later occasions, I talked with her at length about Jesus Christ, explaining the basics of the gospel. She soon received Christ into her own life after an evening meeting.

"Lord," I said, "it is really good to see these friends again. What about Sandy? Whatever happened to her?"

"Sandy is here," the Lord answered. "She is watching your judgment with keen interest, as are many others, because you were instrumental in changing the whole course of her life."

I was shocked. "Changing the whole course of her life? I really didn't do anything, Lord."

"You did, Daniel," he answered. "You were responsive to me. I prompted you to reach out to her, and you did. Sandy went on to become a very significant leader in her church and community. At the time of your calling to the heavenlies, she was thirty-four years old, a wife, and the mother of three children. After her teenage years, she became a leader of campus ministries at her university. She also became a godly and loving woman, a teacher of the Scriptures and a discipler of other women. Sandy has not yet faced her own judgment, but when she does, she will be highly rewarded.

"In all this, Daniel, you have had a part. As an adolescent, she was shy and afraid. Your initiative to connect her with others in my body proved to be the turning point in her life. The love and attention you extended to her gave her the courage to pursue the opportunities your church afforded. Your faithful explanation of the good news helped lead her to me. All else followed. Therefore, a portion of the rich rewards she will receive is yours. She eagerly anticipates the completion of these judgments in order to thank you personally for the impact you made in her life."

My knees almost buckled. Here I discovered what was possibly the greatest surprise of the Bema judgment: I found that the heaviest burden to bear was the Lord's approval. To learn the real truth about oneself—to know all without illusions—and then to be commended by him took all my strength away. With all the truth I had learned about myself, I did not know if I could shoulder the incredible fact of being important in the life of someone else.

In fact, it caused me to wonder if the degrees of glory awarded at the Bema might also be an issue of capacity. In the judgments I had seen, even the greatest, most highly honored saints appeared crushed by the experience of viewing their lives through the Lord's eyes. Perhaps only the greatest of souls are granted the highest degrees of glory, because only they are capable of bearing the weight.

The Lord's approval of this small matter in my past felt like a great burden. "But Lord," I said, "it was not anything big that I did."

"Neither is a cup of cold water given in my name, and yet I will remember it," he answered. "Remember, Daniel, that a great tree can grow from a very small seed. Small actions of obedience done by faith in me can sometimes bear fruit of great proportions."

"But Lord," I said again, "I tried teaching the Bible to a small group on a few occasions, and though it was beneficial, I wasn't very good at it."

"It is true, Daniel, that your gift was not teaching," said the Lord. "Your gift was actually encouragement, which could be exercised in many ways. You employed your spiritual gift on that occasion through serving as a group leader. On many more occasions you encouraged people in informal ways in the normal course of life. Sometimes, what seemed to you to be a plain, ordinary conversation was actually a very significant event to someone else. You encouraged others to seek to know me in a more intimate way, or to persevere by faith in hard times. Your gift was a valuable one, with the potential to make a great impact in my service."

Looking again at my teenage self, I experienced the inexpressible joy of knowing ... *knowing* that here were times and actions the Lord looked upon with approval. At that period of my life, I sincerely desired to yield myself to Jesus Christ as a willing servant. I sincerely and regularly searched his Word—to learn the truth, certainly, but also just for the sheer pleasure of meeting with him. My relationship with him was the chief desire of my heart and the joy of my life. Serving was then a natural outgrowth of that relationship, a pleasure to perform.

This is no claim to sinlessness or perfection. I never lived a sinless twenty-four hours in my life. But as he reminded us, God looks on the hearts of men. He is pleased by an inner attitude of faith expressed through obedient actions done in dependency upon him. Here was another surprising lesson of the Bema. On earth I was aware that he would one day judge his people, burning up the "wood, hay, and stubble," and retaining the "gold, silver, and precious gems." But I thought those two categories symbolized evil, sinful actions on the one hand, and good, worthy actions on the other. I discovered that real life doesn't actually fall into such neat categories. The wood, hay, and stubble category, I discovered, does not refer only to positively *evil* actions, but it is broader. It means those things that are worthless. An action outwardly good could be judged worthless by the Lord because of selfish or hypocritical motives on the part of the servant. I also learned that actions considered gold, silver, and precious gems were never completely pure.

In fallen men, even our best actions are tainted. Our purest motives contain traces of self-interest or pride. I could, for example, give some money to a needy person. I could honestly say that my dominant motive was to do an act of kindness. But I don't think I ever did such a thing without a small part of my heart chiming in, "And what a fine fellow I am to have done so! I hope someone was watching." Or, I could have been leading a small group Bible study, as I did many times when I was younger. I could honestly say that my dominant motive was to point to the Lord and the truth of his Word so that people might be drawn to more intimate faith in him. But it could be equally true that, even as my mind was thinking and my mouth was speaking the truth of the Scriptures with all sincerity, there was another small part of my mind thinking, "And that girl in the easy chair has great legs. I wonder what she thinks of me?"

It just isn't that simple that believers do good or bad works. Therefore, as fire purifies precious metals—burning away the dross, the worthless contaminant—the fire of the Lord's judgment is intended to burn all impurities away from our worthy actions so that they will be truly pure.

His fire continued to burn, and the value of my life became increasingly exposed.

CHAPTER 18

⤳

While I was in college, my spiritual maturing made progress for a while. Three or four friends on my Freshman floor, including Jerry, were believers, and we tried to encourage one another. We participated in some of the campus ministries available, and I continued to study the Word. Unfortunately, my dedication was not as deep as I thought, and it did not last long.

By the beginning of the second semester my decline had begun. Fraternity rush had come and gone, and I was now a pledge of one of the top three. The social events I attended were less than edifying. At first I was embarrassed just to be physically present at parties where heavy drinking was the center of activity. Like most things, though, familiarity lessened that first reaction. I drank, though in small amounts compared with others, to be sociable. My reluctance must have been obvious to them, and they didn't like it. "C'mon, Mathewson!" the upperclassmen would roar. "Drink it down!" And I would. I should have been aware that my old pattern of seeking the group's approval was reasserting itself, but I was too entranced by being included at the top level of social activity. Having attractive female students of the top sororities watching and laughing at me did not make it easier.

My faith was sincere, but it was not strong enough to resist such pressure. Having been granted entrance to such a level of social acceptance, I was not about to do anything to jeopardize it. I began to drift from associations with other believers, and I opened the Bible less and less often. It made me feel too guilty to read it.

Having forced myself to choke down alcohol (at first, it tasted like gasoline!), I got used to it, then began to like it. Finally, I was behaving just like all the rest.

It was astonishing to me, as I observed, how quickly this decline occurred. With a heavy heart I watched what I knew was coming. I began to go out with girls I never before dreamed would be interested in me. I was electric with excitement, though I willed myself to behave with composure. Temptations assaulted me that I had never foreseen as possible. I was too shy to be an aggressor, but these women were not. They were presenting themselves as willing partners to me. I escaped from those situations for a while, but the inevitable occurred. I became sexually active, as they say.

I said nothing to the Lord as the flame burned over this portion of my life. There was nothing to say. I could only be grateful for the forgiveness and grace that he purchased for me at the price of his own blood.

Months passed, and I continued living a life like those who do not know the Lord. Then, with a stabbing feeling like a dart to the chest, I saw a particular girl named Peggy. I didn't know if I could bear to watch further.

Peggy was a sweet young woman, innocent and guileless. She was a year younger than I, fairly shy, but quite attractive. Unlike most of the women I dated, Peggy reminded me of the better part of myself, the part that wanted to be good. We became steady dates, and many months passed in which we enjoyed innocent fun. Peggy was a virgin and didn't drink, and for a time she drew my behavior up to her level. She looked up to me and valued my opinion of things. Often, our conversation would drift into the spiritual realm, and I would tell her what the Bible said. During those conversations, I felt that I was almost awakening from a deep sleep. It felt refreshing to recall what I knew of the Scriptures, and a little of my joy in Christ returned. I prayed a little more often, and began to open my Bible again.

It was a short-lived improvement. My lusts were stronger than my spiritual desires. Little by little, I pulled Peggy down to my level. Through my example and influence she tried alcohol. She would only sip at first, but later developed a strong taste for wine. Over the months, we progressed gradually from fairly innocent kissing to making out heavily. I told her that I would in no way influence her to have sex, and we always stopped just before that point. By the end of the year, she no longer stood out among her sorority sisters as refreshingly different; her attitudes and behavior were pretty much like the majority.

Finally came the night that I dreaded watching. I was studying alone in my room, when I received a phone call from her telling me that she was coming over. She arrived in a somewhat giddy mood. She had apparently been drinking some wine before coming. "I've made up my mind," she said. "I've decided that it's time to lose my virginity, and you're the one whose going to do it."

"No," I said. "I told you before: that's not something you do in the pressure of the moment. It's too big a decision, and I don't want to be responsible for it."

"It's not on the spur of the moment," she replied, smiling. "I've been thinking about it for a long time, and tonight's the night."

The better side of my mind continued to shout "No!" but the voice got weaker. I protested to her for a while longer, but before I knew it we were kissing. There was no more meaningful resistance.

Our relationship began to go sour. The innocent fun, friendship, and conversation we once enjoyed seemed to dissipate like smoke. All that remained were the enjoyments of the flesh. A relationship that had been growing into something really good collapsed into chaos. Conflicts began to emerge. Jealousies sprang to life. We stopped dating two months later, just as the school year ended. Peggy did not return the following semester.

"Oh, Lord..." I began. I did not know what to say. Once again I had been an important influence, a turning point in someone's life. But this time, in the wrong direction. "Lord, what happened to Peggy? Did she go on to have a happy life?"

"Peggy experienced many troubles," he answered. "She never continued her education, and drinking became a serious problem for her. She eventually married three times. The first for five years, after which her husband abandoned her. Second, for three months, after which she left because her husband physically abused her. She was still married to the third, who treated her well, when I came for the Church. Ten years after you knew her she became a believer and she is here at this time."

She is watching me now? I thought. What must she think of me?

"I am the cause, aren't I, Lord?" I said. "I caused the suffering in her life."

"No," the Lord Jesus replied. "You are not the cause of her choices. Every individual is responsible for his or her own sins, but all of you served as important influences on one another. You could be a guide and leader to help one another along the path of salvation and the experience of abundant life. Or, you could be a stumbling block, an occasion or source of temptation, over which others could fall to their own injury. But you are not responsible for someone else's sin.

"Do not think, Daniel, that this sin was worse than the others because of the direction her life took. The other sexual relationships in which you were involved were just as wrong, though the results are not so apparent to you. Those other women were already pointed in that direction when you encountered them. In those cases, your fault was not that you helped turn them that way, but that you had opportunity to represent me and influence them in the right way, but did not."

I thought for a moment about all this. "What would have happened, Lord, if I had behaved differently? What if I had been faithful to be what you wanted me to be? What if I had resisted temptation with Peggy?"

"Almost all questions will be answered in the heavenlies," replied the Lord, "but not that question. The one thing you can never know is what might have been.

Even the shoulders of glorified saints are not strong enough to bear that knowledge. What actually was and what is will be burden enough."

I returned my attention to the unfolding of my life. The way my relationship with Peggy ended soured my stomach toward the lifestyle I had been living. I returned my focus to the Lord, and my behavior improved over the remainder of my time at the university. I studied more diligently, and was moving well toward a Bachelor's degree in Business Administration.

Then, with great delight, I saw my first introduction to Susan Kelly. I laughed with pleasure as I saw that gorgeous twenty-one year-old woman who would become my life partner.

We were a great match. We began dating the last month of my senior year, and continued for another eighteen months before marrying. Susan was a dedicated Christian, but not a stuffy one, and she made me a better man. She laughed loud and liked to have fun. "Coloring outside the lines" was her philosophy of life. Her brain was better and quicker than mine, but she didn't try to dominate me. She merely wanted to be the best partner she could be, and I believe, in hindsight, that she achieved her goal.

Watching the early years of our marriage speed by was very enjoyable. Susan and I had loads of fun, then began to have children and had even more fun. Mark was born, then Janie, then Jeffrey. My heart almost broke with joy and thanksgiving as I watched myself and my wife being blessed with children, gifts of God beyond description. We were faithful members of our church. Susan helped in a variety of ways with her servant's gift, and I helped teach children's and youth Bible studies.

My life again became hard to watch. The weaknesses in my soul began to cry out for gratification. We were quite happy living modestly, but I began to grow dissatisfied. The people I rubbed shoulders with in business were living at a level far above ours. I wanted more, and I started to pressure Susan to help.

She was cooperative at first, having plenty of brains and talent to employ. She began to work part-time at a local business, and quickly worked her way into management. She struggled to keep her involvement at a part-time level, but the owners wanted more and more of her. Susan didn't like it, and often complained that her first priority was to be a mom. To be honest, I didn't mind. Her higher income would allow us to move up in the world.

I wish I could say I didn't know how much it hurt her to miss out on the children's lives as much as she did, but it would not be true. I knew. I just chose to ignore it. I left her alone to deal with the pressure.

How could I do that to her? I truly loved this woman God gave me. It broke my heart to watch. I owed her more than I could ever say. No man could ever ask for a better partner, and yet I was only locked in on my personal ambitions.

How did I ever get to such a place? Standing at the Bema, I knew that I was about to find out.

CHAPTER 19

᭰

"**S**o ... *Mathewson*." The silky voice of Derek Hogan spoke with emphasis. "Do you think you have what it takes to work for Hogan, Jeter, and White?" He flashed his black eyes and grinned at me, revealing his perfectly formed, perfectly white teeth.

I watched this scene from my past with apprehension. The course of my life was about to make a sharp turn, and I now knew the direction was not positive.

Sitting that day at a secluded table in the most exclusive country club in our city, I felt very differently. The ship I always longed for had come in. My ego was intoxicated by the pursuit of the most powerful software and consulting firm in town. There at the same table were Derek Hogan himself (the driving force), Gerald Baker (the technical wizard), and even Ed White (the legal arm).

It would have been obvious to an objective observer that this triple-team was overkill, intended to overwhelm the candidate with flattery, but I was completely under their spell. The presence of White made it even more remarkable in hindsight. The other two I have already introduced in this narrative, but White and I seldom crossed paths even after I went to work there. He was a darkly mysterious figure at the firm, and seldom interacted with anyone but Hogan.

"Business Law" might have been the official label for Ed White's concentration, but he really specialized in Getting Things Done. How he did it was almost never known, even to his inner circle, but he somehow always found a way to implement the will of Derek Hogan. He thus picked up the nickname, "The Puppeteer" (though not to his face). The company might be embroiled in a legal tangle, when suddenly one day it was all settled, usually decisively in our favor. "How did that happen?" one person would ask. Another would simply smirk and whisper, "The Puppeteer." No further explanation was necessary. After a while, no one had to speak the nickname anymore. The answer became a slight tugging motion with one's wrist, simulating the pulling of strings.

But despite the quiet power and mystery of White and the impressive technical knowledge of Baker, Derek Hogan commanded all attention wherever he was. Face to face at an intimate dining table, he seemed the most magnetic and dynamic man I had ever met. And Derek Hogan was pursuing me to join his company and work closely with him! I had to use all my mental and emotional will-power to carry on an intelligent conversation.

That's how I felt that day. All things looked remarkably different at the Bema. At the Judgment Seat of Christ, the truth, the true value, and the true proportion of all things were revealed. I had seen a triumphal procession of great and wonderful saints of God go to the platform to receive their evaluations. I had seen the Lord Jesus Christ, the Sovereign Lord of all creation, commend them for their lives and devoted service to him. I had seen the awesome rewards he bestows on his faithful ones. Now, in comparison to these, I saw again Derek Hogan. I saw that in God's sight he was nothing, and less than nothing—chaff to be blown away in the wind. Next to the genuine greatness of souls I had seen in the heavenlies, Hogan and the others looked like small, oily lizards. Why had I been so taken in by appearances?

That day at the dining table, however, I thought I had achieved the pinnacle of my life. Now looking on from the perspective of the Bema, it was like watching a fly hovering around the attractive appearance of a venus flytrap, entranced by its fragrance. Though I knew it was irrational, I wanted to cry out to myself, "No! Don't listen to them!" I could only watch.

I had graduated from college with my business degree. Like most young men, I was brash and egotistical, not mature or experienced enough to know what I didn't know. Even so, John Mischell decided to give me a chance. Mischell & Associates, only a few years old, was a fledgling software and consulting firm. John had known me since I was a child, being a friend of my father, and he was mature and wise enough to look past my youthful rough edges. He was a good man—too good, I thought, to be very successful in business. Over the many years we worked together, I often complained that he was not aggressive or cut-throat enough. He always smiled and said, "Maybe not. But I'm comfortable with the way we do things."

John got in early on the computer wave of the 1980s. At that time, numerous businesses realized they needed to computerize their systems, but had no one on staff who knew anything about it. Most were scared stiff of computers. John Mischell and his original three assistants had the know-how to recommend the hardware and systems a company needed and the skill to teach people how to implement them, but they were poor in marketing themselves. That's where I came in. Beyond knowing enough to talk about it adequately, I never understood very much of the technical side of computers or software. But it became evident over time that I had a knack for selling and deal making. I understood the mentality and unspoken questions of the average businessperson, and had the ability to translate into language he understood what our systems would do for him and how they worked. John and I, therefore, made a great team.

Mischell & Associates grew at a steady and healthy pace for the next decade, adding employees and making a good profit (though not nearly what we could have made, as I frequently reminded John). Even though I sincerely believed in the quality of our products and service, I got tired of always being the underdog. It was fun on occasion to sneak up on the big boys and take away an account they thought they had won. I even won a few from under the nose of Hogan, Jeter & White. But it was tiring always to be David taking on the Goliaths of business.

John made sure I was well rewarded—at least, by the measuring stick of how our company as a whole was doing. My family was provided for, and more, and I liked everyone in our office. It was a healthy, friendly place to work. They were good people to work with, they were positive, and there was a team atmosphere. But I little appreciated it at the time. What we were making was not enough! I badgered John to be harder on them, to insist on more ambitious goal setting and more production.

"Dan," he said, "they *are* working hard. They *are* setting goals and attaining them. They *are* producing. They are a great bunch of people. What more could we want out of them?"

I didn't answer him then, but now at the Bema I knew the true answer. I just wanted *more*. More what? Fill in the blank. More of everything, especially for me.

In the searching flame of the Lord's eyes, another ugly secret was exposed, one I kept carefully hidden and never mentioned to a living soul on earth: I wanted recognition. No … wanted is too weak. I *lusted* for it. And I knew I would never get it at Mischell & Associates. I kept my thoughts carefully hidden, but I positively hated the smug disdain I received from representatives of the Goliath firms. When I made a new acquaintance at a business gathering, there was the inevitable question: "Who do you work for?" I always smiled and answered in a confident tone, while inwardly bracing myself for the reaction. He might have never heard of us. Or, there was a vague flicker of recognition in the eyes, and a kind word. Or, worst of all, a serious-sounding compliment while his eyes betrayed amusement and condescension. It made me feel like I was wearing little boys' short pants in a room full of tuxedoed adults.

I wanted to be one of the Big Boys. I wanted my name to be attached to a name that made people sit up and take notice. And, of course, I wanted the level of financial rewards that went with being on the highest shelf.

It was this secret lust that was really behind my criticism of John Mischell. It was also the secret motivation behind my leaving the firm.

I did not then have the advantage of hindsight. Not until after I had been at Hogan, Jeter & White for several months did I begin to learn the truth about how others regarded my former company. I never engaged in a specific conversation about it, but stray comments from co-workers told me what I would never have guessed: that Mischell & Associates was highly respected as a competitor. Though much smaller and less diversified, in head-to-head competition they were considered a knowledgeable and formidable opponent. Along with this, their ethical reputation was beyond reproach (a direct result of the reputation and influence of John Mischell), making them even tougher to negotiate against. An associate told me on one occasion, "I'm really glad you're on our side if we have to go up against Mischell." Why had I been so blind to the reality around me?

But blind I was, and no such thoughts entered my mind when I received that surprise phone call from Derek Hogan.

"I've heard about you," he began, sending a thrill up my spine. "I understand you are doing very well at your present company, and you may be perfectly happy there. But I am always looking for brains, talent, and ambition. Are you interested in a conversation?"

With my heart thumping so hard I was afraid he'd hear it over the phone, I managed to answer in what I hoped was a businesslike voice, "Yes, I would be interested in talking." He named the time and place, and I managed to hang up the receiver.

That's how I came to find myself sitting in the dining room of our city's most exclusive country club. Besides the business discussion for which we had met, the lunch was interesting for the different personalities involved. Gerald Baker was a jovial, unbusinesslike bear of a man. He would have made a good class clown in another setting, I thought. After observing the odd contrast he made next to his superiors, I decided that Hogan must tolerate him solely for his technical contribution. Ed White mostly scowled and stared into space when he wasn't looking at me with dead, expressionless eyes.

Derek Hogan was all charm. While he did not exactly tell jokes, he seemed in a constant state of slight amusement. The effect produced conversation that had the tones, smiles, and volume of good humor and camaraderie, but there was an unmistakable undertone of danger. "You may smile and laugh with me," it said, "but I may tear your jugular without warning." He was like a man-eating tiger: beauty, power, and danger in a single fascinating package.

All I could see that day as we talked was the Hogan rocket racing toward the financial stratosphere, and I had the chance to hitch a ride. He casually mentioned a starting salary fifty percent higher than I was making, with the opportunity to make bonuses based on production. "Oh, yes," he added. "You realize that I'm not promising anything, but for proven performers there is the chance of sharing in the partnership one day." That prospect was beyond my ability to imagine, too far from reality for my mind to take in.

That's when he dropped his final question: "Do you think you have what it takes to work for Hogan, Jeter, and White?"

I was already sold. The only question in my mind was, "Can I start today?"

What I actually said was, "Yes, I do, Mr. Hogan. I know my business and I work hard. If I decide to accept your offer ..." (emphasis on *if*. I didn't want to appear too eager or green behind the ears) "... you will be glad you signed me for your team."

Hogan sat back in his chair and stared at me with a serious expression. Then he grinned and extended his hand. "All right, Mathewson. It's a good idea to think things over. How much time do you need?"

"I'll tell you in forty-eight hours," I answered confidently.

It was a grim sight to watch myself from the Bema. I knew that the foolish young man I was watching actually thought he had impressed Derek Hogan. I really thought that Hogan and the others shared the high opinion I had of myself. I had no thoughts at the time of John Mischell or the others with whom I had worked for many years. I had no thoughts of any obligations I might owe John or his company.

The four of us stood and I shook each one's hand. The three of them were going to stay and talk further, so I turned to leave. "Just one more thing, Mathewson," said Hogan. His black eyes were serious, and he was definitely not smiling. "There's one thing I want you always to remember: Bucks is the name of the game. Don't ever forget it."

I looked him in the eye for a few moments, then nodded and walked away.

CHAPTER 20

❧

I didn't need the forty-eight hours to make up my mind. I just needed some time to figure out how I was going to tell John Mischell I was leaving.

I shouldn't have been surprised that John took it graciously. My apprehension was probably due to my own guilty feelings. As I watched from the Bema, John appeared a little sad, though not surprised. His main concern seemed to be for my well being rather than for his company.

"Well, of course, Dan," he said. "I hate to lose you. You're like family to me, and you've helped build this whole company. But I don't want to stand in your way, if this is something you want to do." He said the last phrase with a very slight questioning tone. It was clear that he had doubts. He shook my hand.

"Thank you, John," I said, smiling and friendly. "My years here have been great, and I wouldn't trade the

experience for the world. But I just … you know …"
There was a moment of silence.

"I understand," John said. "You're still young and ambitious, and this is your chance to make a jump to bigger
stakes."

"Yeah, that's right," I said. My broad smile spoke as
much of my relief that there wouldn't be a scene as it did
that I was being freed to follow my desires. After that rush
of relief, though, I became concerned not to appear too
happy. I went on to speak of my appreciation for the years
I had spent with John and how much valuable experience I
gained through more than a decade at Mischell &
Associates.

We talked awhile, and the tone became more relaxed
and friendly, almost nostalgic. But there was one more important issue to discuss, one of which I was especially
fearful.

I think John knew there was something; in fact, he
probably knew exactly what it was. I hesitated, frowning. I
looked down and shuffled uncomfortably, and I believe I
would have begun kicking dirt clods around had I not
been in a carpeted office. I looked to my watching self like
a little boy caught raiding the cookie jar.

"Is there anything else?" John asked, having taken a
seat behind his desk. He looked very formidable to me at
the time.

"I suppose there is one other thing we should talk
about," I said. "I'm not exactly sure what my duties will be
at Hogan, Jeter, and White …" (I tried to tell myself at the
time that this was not exactly a lie, but in the light of the
Lord's truth there was no denying the attempted decep-
tion) "… but it is possible that I'll be working in an area

where I'll be competing with Mischell and Associates." I halted, hoping against hope that John would help me.

He did. "Are you speaking of a non-compete agreement?"

"Yes," I answered, feeling greatly relieved.

John sat back in his chair and folded his hands in front of his chest. He looked me in the eye, and said, "We've never had a contract, Dan. We've tried to treat one another with fairness and integrity. What do you think is right?"

I didn't like having the ball hit back into my court. "I don't know, John." I shrugged, "I've never done this before." I gave a little nervous laugh, but I did not feel now as I watched this scene that there was anything even the slightest degree funny.

"I think the standard tends to be three years," John said after a moment's thought. "You agree that you will not personally deal with customers who have contractual agreements with Mischell and Associates for three years. After that, you are totally free. Is that fair?"

I was actually very disappointed then that John was going to adhere to the common industry standard, but I said, "All right. I promise." I had hoped that he'd be softer. But it would be okay, I thought. Mischell & Associates was a little fish, and where I was going we didn't need to go after such small pickings.

We shook hands, and I gave my word to John Mischell. I would not deal with customers already under contract with his company.

What a hypocritical performance! I thought in grim self-evaluation. If my resurrected body had been capable of it, I would have gotten sick to my stomach from watching the selfish manipulation I was trying to pull off. As the Lord and I began to walk through these last few years of my life, I knew there would be little light and life ahead. I knew this recent history very well, and it was a downhill slide. I braced myself to observe disagreeable and disturbing behavior.

During my first months at Hogan, Jeter & White, however, I felt like I was on top of the world. Every hour felt more high-powered and energizing than I ever felt at Mischell & Associates. It was like a drug, and I began to lose focus on everything else. My income did jump, and within six months Susan and I had bought a dramatically bigger house. I was in such a state of euphoria at the time that her early complaints about my work hours did not register in my consciousness. I didn't mind going in earlier or staying later, because it was so stimulating to work and see the kind of results we were seeing. The Bible I used to read in the morning and at odd moments during the day began to gather dust. I began to go weeks without seeing the children before school in the morning, and I often missed seeing them before they went to bed at night. None of these were the result of conscious decisions. They were simply by-products of the intensity of my focus.

From the perspective of the Bema it was especially distasteful to observe, but much of the charge I was getting from work was from the personal contact I enjoyed with Hogan and the others of the higher circle. I was getting *in*. More and more, they were admitting me to that fellowship where the whole world was analyzed, plotted against, and attacked for profit. The drive of those people was incredible. I wondered how they could sustain such intensity, but they did month after month. I found that I was beginning to live and work according to their cadence, too, the more

I was around them. Hogan also began to take me along to meetings and socials with the highest power brokers in our city. I dined with the mayor. I ate lunch with council members. The city manager was an e-mail correspondent. Major real estate developers called me for consultations. I was given luxury box tickets to major league baseball, NFL football, and NBA basketball. One of the few perks Susan enjoyed was the platinum level symphony tickets I brought home to surprise her. Many influential people were interested in courting the fast-rising young man touted by Derek Hogan.

The time passed by quickly—one year, two years. I decided again that we deserved a better home, and we moved once more to a larger house; this time, truly stretching even our new income to the limit. Because of the financial demands, I began to subtly and not so subtly push Susan more into the workplace. She seemed to like it, but she always exhibited a vein of sadness. From the Bema it was much more obvious. She was working more hours, not to please herself, but me. Her life became much more hectic and frustrating because of the heightened demands of work and children she juggled, while receiving less help from me, her supposed partner. I was greatly increasing the heat in her life while doing nothing to help her deal with the pressure.

All these things I could only watch helplessly. They were now my personal history, the story of my life as I had written it. No matter how much my values had changed, no matter how differently I now felt about my decisions, at the Bema I could only witness my life as it actually was. Then came the black day from which I could never shake free, the day that haunted me the rest of my time on earth.

Hogan called me into what I thought was a routine managers' planning meeting. There twelve of us sat around a large conference table in a richly furnished room. Everything spoke of opulence: the mahogany table, crystal glasses, china sets, original paintings on the walls. Derek Hogan always did things first class, and those items served as continual reminders of what we were working for.

"Our software sales and service division is underperforming," Hogan said bluntly. We were all taken off guard, since we had exceeded our goals already for the quarter. No one, however, was foolish enough to contradict him. "I'm glad," he continued after a moment, "that no one is going to give me any asinine comments about meeting your goals. Goals are only intermediate check points. Real production is measured by doing *everything* you can do, and believe me, we can do a lot more!"

Everyone listened in silence. This was no discussion group; no arena for trendy team management concepts. Derek Hogan was simply going to tell us what he wanted done, and our job was to do it.

He began to go around the table giving instructions to each department head. He wanted a new software package completed six weeks earlier than projected. He wanted 15% greater profit margin built into another product. He wanted our costs lowered by 10% in another department.

Most of the department heads were used to this kind of approach. Gerald Baker, for example, never flinched. He didn't even seem to lose his good humor, though he had the sense to keep it under wraps. He just nodded agreeably and wrote down the instructions. As Hogan worked his way around the table, it appeared I would be last.

Finally Hogan came to me. "And you, Mathewson," he said, pointing, "you're the best thing going around here." I nearly fell off my chair with surprise. "Your department is climbing fast, and serves as a model of how all departments should be run. Your people are producing and you're doing it right. About the only thing I have to say to you is keep on doing what you're doing."

I was too shocked to react in any way. Out of the corner of my eye, I could see the others looking at me with a variety of expressions, from envy to surprise to admiration. In that instant of time, I felt I had reached the highest plateau. There was no hurdle left between me and the pinnacle of success. It was straight to the finish line from here, I thought.

"There is *one* thing, Mathewson," said Hogan, bringing me back to the moment. "We're producing and we're making profits, but I'm getting tired of how some third-rate companies are getting business that should be ours. Take Metro Century, for example. Why don't we have their business? I want it, and I want you to get it."

A freezing wind blew a dark shadow across the fantasy I enjoyed just a moment earlier. Metro Century was the second largest commercial real estate and development company in town. I had sold them on Mischell & Associates myself, securing the largest contract that company had ever won.

"Well?" insisted Hogan, as his and eleven other pairs of eyes bore in on me.

"Right," I flatly said. I was mentally sobering up quickly.

I didn't hear much of the rest of the meeting. After it broke up I lingered behind. "Derek, may I talk to you for a minute?"

"Yes, but make it quick," he said.

"You already know that I'm willing to work hard and get the job done," I began. Hogan made a face indicating impatience. "But there may be a problem with Metro Century." Hogan's raised eyebrows spurred me to talk faster. "I have a non-compete agreement with Mischell, which doesn't expire for almost a year. Since I originally signed the Metro Century deal for them, I can't personally go after it now."

"You never told me you had a non-compete contract!" Hogan barked.

"Well, it's not exactly a contract," I stammered. "It's just an agreement between me and John Mischell."

"Do you mean it's only a casual verbal agreement?" Hogan pressed.

"Yeah, I guess so," I answered. I hoped with all my soul that Hogan would not say what I knew he was going to say.

He did. "Then there *is* no contract!" he laughed. "White and his department will tear it to pieces if it's challenged, which Mischell is probably not stupid enough to do."

"But …" I was making one more attempt to hold out. "It *is* an agreement, and I owe them something for all the years I worked there."

Hogan grew darker and stepped back. "Okay, Mathewson. You want to go back to playing with toys, that's fine with me. You're here because I thought you had potential. You have the chance to live and work where living and working is worth the effort. You have the chance to know the right people and have the right platform to reach for real power. But if you want to flush it all away because your previous loser boss played on your emotions, then fine. Quit wasting my time." He turned to go back to his office.

In an instant, the whole life I had begun to enjoy—mayors, celebrities, luxury boxes, all of it—threatened to blow apart.

"Wait!" I said sharply. "I didn't mean that." I hesitated, inwardly panicking. "I just *felt* ..." (my mind was racing as if my life were at stake) "... that I *owed* it to you, that you know about that ... *discussion* I once had with John Mischell. I mean, *in case* it ever became a problem."

Hogan seemed to relax, then he grinned. "All right, Mathewson! I *hoped* that I wasn't wrong about you. You're going to do all right. Get after it." I was dismissed.

In the next few months, I did go after the Metro Century account, taking advantage of the positive relations I had built a few years earlier. We did end up taking over their business, and I did very well financially from the deal.

I also stepped over a line I swore I would always maintain. I broke my word to John Mischell.

My entire life during this phase seemed to be going up in one massive conflagration, as the flame of the Lord's eyes torched all that was unworthy of a child of God. I did not expect to find anything that endured among the ashes.

CHAPTER 21

❧

There is nothing much to report from the rest of my life before the Lord called us. I continued to work hard, and I continued to make more money than I ever thought possible. I continued to perform at a furious pace; in fact, I may have turned it up a few notches in an effort to quiet the nagging voice of my conscience and the sour feeling in my stomach. The face of John Mischell haunted my imagination.

I was *in*, all right. Increasingly, I was admitted to the inner circle. To my surprise, I discovered that there was an inner circle within the inner circle. Hogan began to include me in discussions in which the department heads—those who I had thought *were* the inner circle— were talked about as if they were pawns on a chessboard. Even Gerald Baker, I discovered, was not a member of the real circle. I met the hyper-secretive Jonathan James Jeter, the ultimate financier behind our firm, whom practically nobody ever saw.

At first I was electric with excitement. My ego was a mile wide, and I felt like I had conquered the world. But getting *in* turned out to be nothing like I had imagined. Once in, it was not exciting; if anything, it was a let down. I had expected the inner circle to be where great intellects and talents operated at warp speed, and life was lived at full tide. I would learn the secrets of real power.

It proved to be depressingly mundane. Seen up close on this level, Derek Hogan was anything but stimulating. His conversation never drifted beyond acquisitions, deals, and bucks, unless he was speaking sarcastically or critically of other people. I still had enough sense to know that if he talked about everyone else behind his back, then surely he would talk about me behind mine. I learned to distrust him, and began to guard myself and my conversation carefully—both in his presence, and with others who might talk. Hogan had informants everywhere.

Though I was disappointed with the quality of life on the inner circle, I was definitely not disappointed with the perks that went with being there. Hogan was exultant about my securing Metro Century, and he made sure I was tangibly rewarded. More money and more recognition followed. The governor of our state once called me, because "as Derek Hogan's close associate," he thought I might be able to help work out a local problem for him. Surprisingly, I wasn't very impressed. In the end, I liked the money a lot, but being a big shot didn't turn out to be as much fun as I thought it would be.

Finally came the last day of my life as I had known it. I watched as I threw a temper tantrum in my car on the way to the office, as I arrogantly snubbed two wonderful saints of God, Joe Thesecurityguard and Juanita the cleaning woman—neither of whose shoes I was worthy to shine—and ignored the needs of a hurting person, Mary Lou Bernet. All I was concerned about during my last day on planet earth was earning more dollars. That day, like most of the ones before it, went up in smoke.

My judgment was complete. I awaited only the final evaluation of the Lord Jesus Christ.

I stood in silence for a few moments. The Lord looked at me, his face no less kind than before. "The days of your life are complete, Daniel," he said. "This is my assessment.

"You have been rich. I do not mean simply money, though you have indeed been financially rich. I mean rich in the sense of gifts and opportunities. You were given a wonderful foundation of family: a mother and father who knew me, and who guided you to know me. Your basic childhood needs of food, shelter, and protection were abundantly met, unlike multitudes of others who were needy. You received an education, good health, and an adequate mind. Though you were never content, you actually enjoyed greater monetary wealth than the vast majority of human beings in the history of the world. Kings in other generations lived less luxuriously than you did. Even so, you used almost none of your wealth for larger purposes. You could have helped the needy. You could have helped advance the gospel and the meeting of human needs through supporting churches, missions, or my faithful servants, but instead you used your wealth merely for your own pleasure.

"By far, the most important gift you were given was eternal life. You received salvation as an adolescent, and had twenty-five years from that point in which to serve me. Many advantages were given you to nurture that life. Many of my faithful servants attempted to build you in your faith: pastors, teachers, servants, fellow believers. Many saints prayed for your growth and well being, far more than you would ever dream. In fact, some of the financial blessings that you, your wife, and children enjoyed were given to you specifically because I answered the prayers of Joseph Robinson and Juanita Perez. Those two saints prayed unselfishly for you and for the state of your soul, and yet, in your pride, you thought them unworthy of notice. This was characteristic of your attitude throughout life, Daniel. You never developed the discernment to know what is truly important, nor to know the relative value of things.

"Your life was not entirely without merit. There were times in which you truly desired to know me and wished to grow into a man of God. There are many people now witnessing your judgment who remember you as one who positively influenced their lives. You did serve me on many occasions to the best of your ability, and those things are worthy of some glory. You did give of your wealth many times, but often with an attitude of pride that poisoned its fragrance. Some of those actions are worthy.

"However, as you now know clearly, there were many more times when you chose to indulge a life of the flesh, often causing hurt to others. There were other lives sent off in evil and injurious directions through your influence. Your self-centeredness blinded you to others around you most of your life."

None of this was disputable. The Lord was exactly right, and, in spite of the sadness I felt, my heart rejoiced in the truth. Here in the heavenlies, I could not stomach even the slightest degree of illusion or lie.

"You have suffered much guilt over the time you broke your word to John Mischell, but there is more to the story than you know. Derek Hogan was testing you, trying to see if you would do wrong in order to gain access to his inner circle. His great satisfaction came less from the acquisition of the contract itself than from the fact that you did what he wanted. He trapped many others the same way. Seldom do people go from habitual honesty to criminal behavior in a single action. But one small step over a moral line leads to another and to another, each one becoming easier than the last. Through small, incremental steps, Derek Hogan drew many others into his net until they were thoroughly compromised legally and morally. Many of his circle were forced to do his will because of chains thus forged. He had targeted you as his next great acquisition."

I was amazed. What a fool I had been! What might I have done next if the Lord had not interrupted everything? Then, thinking of my conduct in the office brought a different issue to my mind.

"Have you a question, Daniel?" the Lord asked.

"Yes, Lord. You have spoken the exact truth. I have seen the results of my influence on many people, but I was wondering about one: What happened to Mary Lou Bernet? I know I was no help to her when she needed it. How shall I speak to her?" I was thinking of later, after the completion of the Bema judgments.

"Mary Lou Bernet is not here," the Lord Jesus said, "for she is not of the Church."

Not a Christian? I was shocked. But … I thought back. We never actually talked about our faith. I just assumed. Mary Lou appeared to be a clean-living, honest person, and it never occurred to me that she was not a believer. I bent over and stared at the floor of the platform in concentrated thought. No wonder she seemed to fall apart! Throughout all that trouble with her child, she had none of God's resources from which to draw. And I didn't help her. I never gave her understanding, sympathy, or a helping hand. And I never gave her the most important thing I could have given: the knowledge of the gospel. I never told her how she could have Jesus Christ in her life and heart, on whom she could trust in her time of need. It never even crossed my mind. I only pushed her to produce and used her to serve my purposes.

I looked up again at the Lord. What a life! I spent most of my time and energy playing with the toys of the world, and despising the things of real value. If there is anything I learned by observing myself at the Bema, it is how little love there had been in my heart throughout my life. So little love!

"Much good seed was sown in you, Daniel. While there are some things worthy of commendation, the majority of the fruit of your life was choked out by weeds and thorns, by the things of the world and the sins of the flesh. You never learned the value of people and your love was small. You exercised only a little faith. Your life is worthy of a little glory.

"You knew me, and at times were open to enjoying some intimacy with me. But I have this against you: that you left your first love."

He continued to look me in the eye. His expression of kindness and his gentleness of voice never wavered, even in speaking the hardest of truths. His grace was overflowing to the end. "Have you anything to say?"

"No, Lord," I answered. I shook my head. "All you say is the truth."

I was completely out of strength. I fell to my knees, with my hands on the platform and my head bowed low.

Then, a lightning bolt surged through my members. I felt as if I had been turned into light itself, as if I had been united with Life itself. The Lord had touched me.

"Arise, Daniel," he said, lifting me to my feet. He did not say, "Well done, good and faithful servant."

"Daniel," he said softly with his hands on my shoulders, "there is no condemnation for those who are in me. You left your first love, but your first love never left you. The old has passed away forever; the new has come! In the ages to come, you will discover the glory of my Father's life and enjoy the wonders of the new creation. You will serve me with multitudes of wonderful saints. From this foundation, you will be able to learn and grow in an endlessly outspreading life. Welcome to your home!"

He turned me to face the assembled saints who stretched outward and upward for miles from the platform. With his right hand on my shoulder, the Lord Jesus spoke: "This is my beloved Daniel Scott Mathewson. Welcome him!" The multitude roared and cheered in love and welcome.

The Lord had not said the words, "in whom I am well pleased."

CHAPTER 22

The greatest joy of which we are capable on earth is only a bare whiff of the real substance in which we bathe when we share the glory of the Lord Jesus Christ. Even the great joy I had experienced so far in the heavenlies was just the tip of the iceberg compared to what I now knew as a glorified saint. True union with God was mine. The fulness of his Life was a great ocean that flowed directly into my being.

While hundreds of millions of resurrected and glorified saints cheered, I flew under my own power back to my seat. I could fly in the same way I had found I could do other things: by forming my desire and applying my will. My new body was a totally responsive, obedient, and submissive servant to my liberated mind, desires, and will. No longer was my mind dominated by the flesh, that is, by the drives of the body and its senses influenced by sin. God had restored the right relation of things in me, and my human soul now indwelt a body of vastly greater capabilities.

I had one immediate desire as I flew. I willed it to be, and knew where to look. Instantly, in the midst of billions of people, I located four special ones. My eyes locked onto Susan, Janie, Jeffrey, and Mark—standing together, cheering for me, and waving. I waved at them triumphantly. None of them had yet gone to the Bema, and I especially looked forward to seeing Susan receive the glory I knew she deserved.

It would have been enjoyable to join them immediately, but the judgments had to continue for many others and there were no spare seats, so I returned to my original place. As I landed, the saints around me greeted me with pleasure and congratulations. My friend Gensuke (who had not yet been evaluated) bowed humbly. "Daniel," he said, "what an honor to know you, and what a pleasure that we have met so soon in the heavenlies! Congratulations."

"Thank you, Gensuke," I said. "It is *my* honor to have met you!" I knew that when Gensuke was rewarded, his glory would outstrip mine by a factor of ten. And yet, his humility was genuine, and he would remain so even after the Lord had richly honored him before all the watching billions.

"May I offer my congratulations, also, Sir," said a voice in my inner ear. "Thank you for the privilege of serving you."

"No, thank *you*, Uriel," I answered. "You have served me in countless ways, and my life was better as a result. Through the judgment I understand now how and when you served me in life, and I owe you much. I look forward to serving with you in the age to come as friends."

Kolael struck the platform with his staff and summoned the next saint, recalling our attention.

As I watched the continuing judgments, it occurred to me how difficult it would be for anyone who had not experienced the Bema to understand why degrees of glory in the heavenlies did not call forth all the responses that would be seen on earth. How could there not be envy and resentment over others more richly honored? How could there not be anger or mourning over lost rewards? How could I, to be more specific, be full of joy having just watched most of my life burn to ashes?

The answer is because we all desired and rejoiced in the truth. When Gensuke later returned to his seat, having indeed received ten times the glory given to me, I knew it to be right. Every ounce of my soul agreed that he was worthy of that honor, and rejoiced in it. Gensuke carried that honor with the same humility that he had before. He continued to speak to me as if I were his superior, and it was no affectation; he really felt that way. When you know the truth about yourself, and you see the truth about others, you would want it no other way.

Therefore, there will be degrees of glory in the eternal state, but no competition. Some will be less glorified than others, but there will be no envy. Some will be highly honored, but there will be no pride. The greatest saints are the humblest; the least are the greatest. The last shall be first. All will be one: one bride of one Lord; one body of one Head. Forever and ever, his body will be a perfectly responsive servant to his will, serving and growing and enjoying his never-ending, ever-expanding life.

No one at the Bema *deserved* any glory in the literal sense of the word. The only thing we sinners ever truly deserved was ultimate, complete banishment from the presence of God. The substitutionary death of our Lord Jesus Christ on the cross was necessary to save us from what we deserved. "Merit" must be understood as a relative term. The Lord may be pleased to grant his people honor and glory for their faithful attempts to serve him, but no one returned from the judgment with any prideful illusions about literally earning rewards. Therefore, dissatisfaction was impossible.

Had the Lord given me the slightest degree of glory beyond what he did, I could not have borne it; again, because I had come to know the truth about myself. All rejoiced in knowing the truth about themselves and in the glory granted them as an outward manifestation of that truth.

The judgments were eventually brought to a conclusion. Susan was honored as I knew she would be. Her loving and serving heart was manifested in beautiful glory, and I knew I was highly honored to have had her as my earthly mate. Mark, Janie, and Jeffrey also were judged. They displayed the relative purity to be expected because of their youth, but they also surprised me by the honor they merited. In all three, there was genuine faith and developing Christian character. Susan had obviously done well in discipling them, because I could claim little credit.

The last saint having been judged, Kolael turned to the seated Lord and bowed. The arena burned like the glory of several billion suns, all concentrated in one place. The Lord Jesus stood, and we all did the same. He turned to face the manifest presence of God and spoke:

Father, the judgments are complete. I
thank you again for these whom you have
given me. Thank you for the glory you
have given me, and thank you for the
glory I was able to grant them. I present
them back to you. May your name be glorified through them and through their service in the ages to come. They are yours, I
am yours, and we await your command to
take your kingdom to earth.

The great voice responded:

It will be soon. It is time for the kingdoms
of the world to become the kingdom of
the Lord and of his Christ. Enter, my children, into the fulness of everlasting life.
The old has passed away, and you have
been born again into the new creation. Rejoice and be glad, for life has begun.

With the speaking of the final phrase, that visible manifestation of the presence of God faded and disappeared
from view. It was no longer necessary, for the eyes and
hearts of us glorified saints could now perceive God without such an aid. We could see God in the same way as the
Lord Jesus Christ could see him. There are no words or
categories with which I can explain to an earthly reader.
We received a "seventh sense" through the consummation
of our union with him, and we will forever know him face
to face.

"Hallelujah!" we cried. "We praise you, Father, Son, and Holy Spirit, and we offer ourselves as willing servants. Command us, and we will do your will."

Kolael struck the platform three times with his staff. "Praise our God, all you his servants," he cried, "and you that fear him, both small and great. And do honor to the bride, the Church which he has purchased with his own blood."

At this I heard as it were the voice of a great multitude, a roar as of a mighty waterfall, a crash like a thousand mighty strokes of thunder. The voice was not from the assembled Church, but from uncounted unseen observers. It said:

> Hallelujah! for the Lord God omnipotent
> reigns! Let us be glad and rejoice, and give
> honor to him: for the marriage of the
> Lamb has come, and his bride has made
> herself ready. And to her it was granted
> that she should be arrayed in fine linen,
> clean and white: for the fine linen is the
> righteous acts of the saints.

"Uriel," I asked, "who are these that speak and glorify God?"

"They are many angels, including those of my order and of other kinds you do not yet know. They are also the souls of redeemed men and women of other ages. They are the saints of the Old Covenant, and the righteous Gentiles of the nations. They are also those martyred saints who have come out of the tribulation. As we have proceeded in the heavenlies, much has happened on earth. Many saints have been born into eternal life during this time, but it is a time of great trouble. All these await their day of resurrection, which will occur when the Lord returns to earth to reign."

I considered what this multitude had said, and understood the image used: As the bride of Christ, our wedding dress, so to speak, is the glory that has been bestowed upon us. I should have anticipated it. Even on earth, every groom wants a beautiful bride, and every bride wants to present herself as beautiful as possible to her groom. Our great gift of love that we can present to the Heavenly Groom on our wedding day is *ourselves*. The qualities of faith, hope, and love that resulted in lives of willing service to him are our gift of gratitude to the One who purchased our redemption. The Lord also wanted a beautiful bride, and he had purified us that we might be so. Now, through that union we will bear fruit for him throughout an everlasting life.

As I looked on the seated Lord Jesus, my senses began to lose their focus. I seemed to be gazing into a bottomless pool of power and glory and life. Though I had no inclination to take my eyes off him, bright streaks shooting across the atmosphere began to demand my attention. Dozens, then hundreds, then thousands of small shooting stars were rocketing from the circumference of the arena toward the center, landing around the Bema. I finally realized what they were. Saints were flinging their crowns, somehow divesting themselves of their glory, and casting it all at the feet of the Lamb of God. A great crescendo of praise and thanks ascended, growing louder with each moment. As they piled higher, the tokens of honor landing around the platform seemed to blend into one, becoming a molten river of glory moving slowly counter-clockwise around the Bema. The entire company of glorified saints began to sing in unison a doxology of praise and honor, in complete self-abandon to the only One who is worthy. I had no crown to throw, but I could offer my sacrifice of praise, and I sang with all my heart.

How long this worship continued, I cannot say. This must have been what Uriel referred to as "deep time." Though I am only a beginner in understanding, I believe we stood at the borders of eternity and gazed into the depths of the Self-Existent God.

Eventually, the Lord Jesus stepped forward to address the assembly. I looked and saw that all the glory and crowns had been restored to their recipients. No one can outgive the Giver of all things. "The time is nearly at hand," he said. "Only a few things remain before we return to earth to establish the kingdom promised by my Father. I will conduct you, my bride, to your new home: the heavenly Jerusalem, that place I have prepared for you. You will see the great and glorious city in which you have a home forever. In the age to come you will have opportunity to serve your God here in the heavenlies, and also with me as the administrative servants of my kingdom. You will be teachers, evangelists, and shepherds of people on earth for a thousand years. The earth will know peace at last. Once on earth, there will be several judgments to perform, after which we will celebrate the great wedding feast. My faithful kinsmen, to whom was promised the kingdom of renewed Israel, will join us, along with many faithful Gentiles. Others yet to be gathered will also celebrate with us.

"After you have opportunity to view the city, you will be called together. You will be assigned to commanders and receive your individual assignments. Now, for the time being, I release you to rejoice and greet one another."

The assembly was dismissed, and what a sight to behold! Many exited by the portals, but far more simply flew into the open air above the great stadium, spreading out into all directions. From a distance, it must have looked like an unimaginably huge fireworks explosion.

There was no question in my mind what I wanted to do first. I flew out to an open area not far away and landed where I knew Susan and the children would be waiting. There they were, beautiful and glorious, bursting with love and joy. We all embraced with enthusiasm, and we were joined by others. There were my mother and father, my grandparents, and several cousins. A great family reunion building by the moment.

After a time, I took Susan by the hand and pulled her aside for a little privacy. "I want to tell you how honored I am to have been your husband," I began, "and I want to ask you to forgive me. I am so sorry that I was not a better one." I could have poured out hours of confessions of my faults and shortcomings, but Susan stopped me.

"I have been waiting," she said, "to ask you to forgive me that I was not a better wife. I now know how often I failed to be the partner I should have been."

We both smiled and stood in silence for a minute, hand in hand. "It was good to say it," she said, "but it is all past and gone. Now, everything is new." Forgiveness is a given between saints in the heavenlies. We were husband and wife for a time on earth, but we are brother and sister for eternity.

Others came by to greet me. My college friend, Jerry, met me with a powerful hug, almost tackling me. That girl from high school, Sandy, came to express her deep gratitude for the impact my life had on hers. The many degrees of glory by which she surpassed mine made it seem a little odd, like an elephant thanking a mouse for its great influence. But I knew she was utterly sincere, and I was further humbled by her graciousness. Even my childhood friend, Jimmy, came by. Then, John Mischell found me, and rejoiced over me as if I were the returning prodigal son.

It was I who sought out Peggy. I hardly had the chance to ask her forgiveness before she was asking for mine. We were fully reconciled within the all-loving embrace of God. Grace was overflowing everywhere in the heavenlies.

She departed to meet others, and I was left alone. "Uriel," I said.

"I am here, Sir," replied my faithful servant and friend. "Shall I assume a visible form?"

"As you wish," I answered. He did, bursting into flame of bright red, with touches of pink and silver. I knew that he was overflowing with angelic joy.

"Let's walk together," I said. "I have some questions I want to ask you."

We observed some interesting things as we walked. We early encountered a small group of saints—seven or eight of them asking questions, listening attentively, and responding with laughter to an animated person at the center. Drawing closer, I recognized him from the Bema. It was the apostle John. He sat on a stone telling stories with relish and humor, as the other saints stood around or sat at his feet on the soft grass. What a place the heavenlies will be, I thought, to get to know people like John! For the time being, however, I decided to pass on.

On our right in a little alcove of trees, we saw one of the more emotional scenes I witnessed. A man was kneeling before a woman. He seemed to be expressing grief, though heavenly grief is not as it is on earth. Apart from God, grief is hopeless, an injury that can never be healed. Not so in the heavenlies, for there is ready forgiveness and healing. But this saint evidently wished to express himself fully to the woman, whose glory was great. She stood in an attitude of kindness with her hand on his head as they spoke. This was obviously a very private scene into which I did not wish to intrude, so I averted my eyes and we turned away.

Uriel must have known of my unspoken question, because he said, "I can tell you what is happening there, Sir. That woman was a slave from the southern United States before your Civil War. That man was her earthly master, and he was brutal and often evil. He had much to confess to her, but she is a great saint and the past will be forever healed and closed."

A little further, we saw two men talking and laughing together with great joy. Uriel looked at them and flashed a rich pink. It was my impression that he was expressing in angelic terms great pleasure (if not amusement). "I know those two, Sir," he said. "They were in opposing armies in the conflict you knew as World War I. Both were dedicated disciples, and yet they fought each other in a brutal war instigated by evil and foolish men. Perhaps you have heard of the 'Christmas Eve Armistice.' The German and British soldiers halted their hostilities when one of them began singing 'Silent Night.' Soon, soldiers from both sides were singing the carol in their own language, and no shots were fired that night. These two soldiers were there. A few weeks later, they encountered one another in a shell crater while on a charge across the field, and they killed each other simultaneously."

I looked on with awe. How different the world will be from now on! Soon the Lord will call us to tour our new home, and then we will join him in the liberation of planet earth!

Could that be our summons? I heard a new kind of sound reaching across the landscape of the heavenlies. But there was something different about this sound than anything I had heard. It was not pleasant. In fact it was the first irritating experience I could recall since our arrival. What *is* that?

Oh, no! Not *that*! No! I don't want to go back!

But it was too late.

It was the obnoxious shriek of my alarm clock.

CHAPTER 23

✌

I reached out to turn off the alarm and fell back in despair. It *can't* be, I protested. It *can't* have been only a dream! I rose to my elbows and wrapped the pillow around my face. I would have given anything, everything to be in the heavenlies again (assuming I had been there at all).

Unlike most mornings, I was instantly awake and mentally alert. I slipped out of the covers and slumped down in an easy chair in the corner of our bedroom. Never in my life did home feel less like home. I felt as if I had been dropped into a completely alien environment. Maybe it wasn't a dream, I thought. Maybe I had been granted a vision. It was certainly unlike any other dream I'd ever had.

I realized with alarm that some parts of the vision were rapidly slipping away from my memory. I could clearly remember that the heavenlies seemed to be in all ways more than earth, but I could not remember how. I remembered that colors seemed more than on earth, but again I could not remember how. I could recall the appearing of the glory of God, but I could no longer visualize what I actually saw, nor even the appearance of the angelic creatures. Worst of all, I could no longer visualize the appearance of the Lord Jesus. All that remained in my mind were bare facts rather than a real memory: that he was glorious beyond measure or description, that he wore the marks of royalty and priesthood, that his voice spoke with irresistible authority well symbolized by a sword proceeding from his mouth. But a mental picture—No. It was gone.

I was frantic, afraid that I would lose it all. I sat for many minutes, mentally rehearsing the entire vision in order and in as much detail as possible. I found with relief that I had no trouble recalling conversations or insights learned. It was only the visual images I could not retain. Perhaps, I decided, now that I was "back" on earth I did not have the mental capacity or categories in which to store what I had seen. Still, it made me profoundly sad and I longed to return to the heavenlies.

I looked at Susan sleeping soundly, and felt a complex of emotions. I felt I loved her as never before, and felt grief that I had not loved her better. I felt humbled that she would love someone like me at all, much less that she would put up with all my nonsense through the years. I clenched my jaw in grim determination. Whatever happens from here on out, it is *not* going to be more of the same!

"Lord Jesus," I prayed, "I would rather be in heaven with you. But if it's your will that I serve a while longer on earth, I want to do it right. I've never been good at making New Year's resolutions. I've broken a thousand promises I made in my own strength, and so I have no hope if I trust in myself. If there's anything I have proven by my sorry performance it is that I can't live a Christian life on my own. But Lord, I'm willing to offer myself to you, if you will do it in and through me. I need your life and your power and your wisdom. I need you to produce the results. If you leave me to myself, I will utterly fail, and I will be a cause of downfall for others. I'm ready to learn and grow, Lord. Please teach me."

I have a lot to do, I said to myself, while getting up and heading for the bathroom. I shaved deliberately, deep in thought. Looking into my eyes in the mirror, I inwardly asked, Okay, Mathewson, what kind of man do you want to be? I think it was the first time I had ever considered that question. I had many times considered what I wanted to accomplish, or what goal I wanted to attain, or how much money I wanted to make. But never, "What kind of man do I want to *be*?" Now I knew that it was immeasurably more important than those other questions.

While showering and dressing, I thought more about my vision/dream (I never have decided what to call it). Especially, I began to think about the first part, before the Lord called us to heaven. The details were essentially right, but the timing seemed confused. What day *is* this anyway? I suddenly wondered. Monday, the same day that my dream began. But some of those things actually happened already. Today is when we are supposed to meet with Wiederman, all right, but it was on Friday that I was preparing to close the deal. It was on Friday that I shared with Baker and Hogan my misgivings, and Hogan came back with the partnership offer.

I felt a powerful mental jolt. What *is* going on around that office? Why is everybody so interested in my signature? There's something really fishy going on. I am going to the office, and I am not going to rest until I find out what it is.

There were a few things left to do before leaving the house. I felt a longing to see my children, and peeked in at each of them as they slept. I'm not worthy to be your father, I told them silently, but with God's help I am going to do better. Then I wrote a note to Susan. It read: "Honey, it would mean a lot to me if we could go out tonight, just the two of us for dinner. I would really like to talk to you. Do you think you could get a sitter on short notice? I would really appreciate it. This is important." Then, "PS: I love you <u>very much!</u>" I put it by her purse, and left the house.

I drove at a moderate speed in the middle lane of the highway, thinking hard, with my mind buzzing from issue to issue: I'm going to have another look at that Wiederman contract. I need to talk to Mary Lou as soon as possible. And I've got to get a look at the testing data for that software. Most of all, I want to get to my Bible! How I'd love to have a whole day to do nothing else but read it! In spite of this rapid mental activity, I felt unusually calm.

I arrived downtown without incident and parked. As I entered the first floor lobby of our building, I hoped to see Joe Thesecurityguard. There he was. "Why, Mr. Mathewson," he exclaimed. "You're awfully bright and early today!"

"Yes I am," I said smiling as I walked over to him. I extended my hand and he shook it. "Tell me how you are, sir," I asked. How foolish I was to have looked at this man in the world's typically stupid way: according to mere externals, such as race, clothing, and speech. I now felt humbled and honored to be speaking personally with this great saint.

"I am doing wonderfully!" he replied. "God is good to me every day. Do you know what the Scriptures say? 'It is of the Lord's mercies that we are not consumed, because his compassions fail not. They are new every morning: great is thy faithfulness. The Lord is my portion, saith my soul; therefore will I hope in him. The Lord is good unto them that wait for him, to the soul that seeketh him.' That's Lamentations three, twenty-two to twenty-five."

I had no doubt he was right. I nodded and listened carefully to the passage he recited. His easy quoting of the Word of God felt to my soul like an oasis of cool water and intensified my desire to read it for myself.

"Is there anything I can do for you, Mr. Mathewson?" he asked.

I had one thought. "Yes, Joe, there is. I have to do some very hard things today, and I need God's help. If you think of it, will you pray for me today?"

Joe seemed pleasantly surprised. "Why, I'd be delighted!" he answered. "I don't know what kind of things you fight against in your world, but we all need the strength of the Lord to fight the good fight. I will most definitely pray for you today and every day."

I thanked him sincerely, and took the elevator to our floor. As I opened my office, Juanita was nowhere to be seen; but I found coffee ready for me in the break room. Without further delay, I took out my Bible and sat down to read.

My memory of the Scriptures was rusty from neglect, so I fumbled a bit, flipping back and forth. I was fortunate that it was the same Bible I had used since college, because

I had written many notes inside that helped me find what I was looking for. Here was one verse:

> For we must all appear before the judg-
> ment seat of Christ, that each one may re-
> ceive what is due him for the things done
> while in the body, whether good or bad.
> (2 Corinthians 5:10)

I had put an asterisk by the words, "judgment seat," and a note in the margin: "Greek: Bema." So *that's* where I learned it. There was also a cross-reference to another passage, 1 Corinthians 3:11-15. It read:

> For no one can lay any foundation other
> than the one already laid, which is Jesus
> Christ. If any man builds on this founda-
> tion using gold, silver, costly stones, wood,
> hay or straw, his work will be shown for
> what it is, because the Day will bring it to
> light. It will be revealed with fire, and the
> fire will test the quality of each man's
> work. If what he has built survives, he will
> receive his reward. If it is burned up, he
> will suffer loss; he himself will be saved,
> but only as one escaping through the
> flames.

There's the description of the Bema judgment, I thought, but I had deeper understanding now. I had lived it. I had seen most of my life burn to ashes in the evaluation of the Lord. Whether it was a dream or vision or whatever, I had been given greater and clearer self-knowledge than ever before. And I didn't like what I had seen.

I meditated on that passage for a time and grew more determined. I have a second chance! As long as God grants me life and breath, I can change. I know I can't change myself alone, but by his grace I will become a man of God.

I got up, locked my office door for complete privacy, and turned off the light. For the first time in many years, I knelt to pray and prayed from the deepest recesses of my heart.

"Lord God. Father in heaven. I'm not competent to know for sure what that dream was. I don't know if it was just a dream, or a vision sent by you. I guess it doesn't really matter. It doesn't matter if the Bema will be just like I dreamed. The main point is, now I know. What I saw about myself is true. It is absolutely true, Lord, how far I have fallen! I have done ugly things, evil things. I have betrayed friends. I have lied. I have used people. I have failed to love or serve people. I have failed to represent you properly or make myself available to serve you. I have served myself instead.

"Lord Jesus, what you said in my dream was true, too. I have left you, my first love. I actually did that a long time ago. Thank you for never leaving *me*! But I want to come back. I want to experience real life, and I know it is only found in knowing you."

My heart and mind were burdened with deep sadness over many of the things in my past, and I struggled with how to put into words the powerful yearning I now felt. It came out this way:

"Lord, life without you is not life. I used to think that getting *in* would be a big deal, a big charge. I found out that it isn't. It's like being really hungry, and being served cardboard to eat."

A strong urge suddenly came over me to stop praying as a wave of fear washed over me. An inner voice sounded an alarm. *Look out! If you pray what you are about to pray, you'll be caught! You're going to lose everything! A little bit of forgiveness and peace is great; but if you get carried away, you'll end up tossing your whole life out the window, everything you've worked to attain!*

It interrupted my concentration for a minute. I felt an inward panic and a strong compulsion to get off my knees before it was too late.

I shook my head, wondering, Where did *that* come from? I immediately knew. It was the voice of evil, of sin, of temptation. I don't know if Uriel has an evil counterpart, but if he does, those are just the kind of ideas he would be expected to suggest. In fact, I thought, I believe I *have* obeyed that voice many times in my life. But not *this* time! With confidence, I resumed praying:

"Father, you know the kind of confusion and lies that are banging around in my head. Please stop them, and help me think clearly about the truth. Lord Jesus, I am a weak man, full of fears and temptations. But this is the truth: I want to be your kind of man. I want to have a life that has eternal value. I want to serve you, and hear you say to me some day, 'Well done, good and faithful servant.' Most of all, Lord, I want to know you. And I'm asking you to make yourself real to me. If what I suspect turns out to be true, and if I do what I think you will want me to do, I may be totally washed up in this world. But that will be okay if I know you."

I thought for another minute, then said, "Lord, I would rather turn burgers at a fast food restaurant to feed my family and know you, than to be the world's biggest and richest tycoon and not know you." I couldn't believe I said it, but I did ... and I meant it.

The fear was completely dissipated. I felt totally confident, even knowing that tough battles lay directly ahead. "I thank you with all my heart, Lord, for your forgiveness, for the acceptance that is mine because I am in Christ Jesus. Thank you for loving me, and thank you for even listening to someone like me. Let my life from now on bring honor to you, and be pleasing to you. My life is in your hands. Show me the way."

I paused, then added with feeling, "I am asking these things in the name of Jesus Christ." I think it was the first time I ever said that phrase with understanding. Always before, it was just a way to end a prayer. Now I knew the truth behind it. Apart from Christ, there is no way a holy God would accept my presence or receive my prayer. But, by faith in Christ's righteousness—that is, all the grace he purchased for us at the cross—and on the basis of *his* merits, I can pray with boldness and assurance that God hears and will answer me! It is a statement of faith in *Christ*, as opposed to a faith in self-righteousness.

I arose from my knees, turned on the light, and unlocked the door. If it is possible for a Christian to be born again again, I was; and I knew it immediately.

But there were difficult challenges ahead, and I didn't yet know what to do. I wondered, where can I get help in the Bible? After a little searching I found the passage I vaguely remembered:

> Trust in the Lord with all your heart and
> lean not on your own understanding; in all
> your ways acknowledge him, and he will
> make your paths straight. (Proverbs 3:5,6)

That's exactly what I've got to do, I thought. Commit myself to the Lord and trust him to give me wisdom as I go, and to plow the road ahead of me through this jungle. I knew there could be personal costs for this road I was choosing, but I felt strangely calm about it. The Lord has promised to meet the needs of his people. A cross-reference helped me find the verse:

> But seek first his kingdom and his righ-
> teousness, and all these things will be given
> to you as well. (Matthew 6:33)

"All right, Lord," I prayed. "I'm going to seek first you and your kingdom, and trust you to take care of the rest. I'm going to try to do right, and trust you to provide for me and my family, whatever happens."

The first day of my new life on planet earth had begun.

Chapter 24

⋧

"Good morning, Mr. Mathewson," said a voice from the door. "I see you found your coffee."

"Yes I did," I said, rising from my chair. "Thank you very much, Juanita. It was very thoughtful of you." I walked around my desk to her and extended my hand. I didn't think it consciously at the time, but my emotions could have been expressed by a question: "How could I *not* rise in the presence of so great a saint?"

"Oh, it is nothing," she replied, with a beaming smile. "Everyone has to work so hard in the world. Little things make it a little nicer."

"Juanita—if you don't mind my asking a personal question—didn't you tell me that you have another job you go to after this one is finished?"

"Yes, I work in a law office, but only till about one o'clock. It's just a small firm."

"And didn't you tell me that you have a child about ready to go to college?"

"Yes. My daughter, Gloria, the last of my four children, wants to go to Tech next fall. She's a very good girl, and probably the smartest of my children." Juanita paused, then added with a sad tone, "She has lots of potential, but Tech is very expensive."

"Haven't you put each of your other children through college before this?" I asked.

"Yes, but they all went to state schools. It was still expensive, but we were able to do it, with me working extra jobs, and the children working to help, too." She smiled. "I'm not worried about it. The Lord is good, and if it's his will, he will provide for Gloria to do whatever she should do."

"What about scholarships?" I asked.

"We'll get some help there, almost for sure," Juanita answered. "Gloria is in the top ten percent of her class, but it still won't be nearly enough."

I nodded thoughtfully. "You're right, Juanita, God is good, and he is very powerful. If he wants it done, it will be."

Juanita answered with confidence, "The Bible says, 'seek first his kingdom and his righteousness, and all these things will be given to you as well.' That's how I have lived for many years, and the Lord has always been faithful to keep his promises." She said good morning and left.

That verse again! There seemed to be a message for me in it. As I watched Juanita walk away, I thought, there goes one brave lady! She has endured more hardship in a year than I have in all my life, and yet she is full of joy and faith. "Lord, may I have just a portion of the courage Juanita has."

I looked at the clock: 7:28 A.M. It was time to go to work.

Normally, I was in a state of high excitement on a day I was working to close a major deal. My heart usually raced and my stomach churned, just like an athlete about to play a big game. But today I felt odd. I felt apprehensive and suspicious rather than excited; confused rather than focused. I needed to do some investigating.

I pulled out the envelope containing the partnership agreement Hogan gave me on Friday, with his personalized sticky note still attached. His note said, "If you can close the deal on Monday, sign these papers and claim your reward."

"*If … If …*" That word seemed to jump out at me in neon letters. In my dream, the note read "this afternoon" rather than "on Monday," but the meaning was the same. The offer of a half-partnership was contingent upon my closing the Wiederman deal. I took a closer look at the contract itself, and a second item seemed to scream for my attention. The contract was dated as of Friday, even though it could not be accepted until Monday. That sure is a strange way of doing things! I thought. What is he up to?

The rest of the contract was routine, nothing odd other than the dating. The more I thought about it, though, Hogan's whole approach seemed even more strange. I was working hard to close this deal anyway, without having this offer. Why go through all this drama? Why did he think I would need any more motivation to do my job?

I next pulled out my draft of the Wiederman contract, and read it carefully. It, too, was standard, nothing obviously unusual. "What is it, Lord?" I prayed. "What is going on around here that is not right? Help me see it."

I continued to pore over the agreement. There were various guarantees of technical support and assertions of thorough testing, but nothing seemed out of line. As I pondered the deal, my mind kept returning to the realization that Henry Wiederman's acceptance or rejection of this agreement would be based on his confidence in my word. Isn't that what Baker had said? "It's because old Henry loves you! You could sell him swamp land in Florida." Is that what Hogan is up to? I wondered. Does he think my participation in this is so critical because I have a reputation for integrity that Wiederman will buy? And does he think I'll need some added incentives to go ahead with it? Why?

People were beginning to drift into the office, so my solitude was over. I was glad, because I needed help to find out what I needed to know.

I walked over to the technical wing of the floor, and was thrilled to see Steven Brunck already at his desk. He was just the person I needed. He was knowledgeable, a key underling to Gerald Baker. Best of all, he was honest and discreet.

"Steve," I said, surprising him. "I need your help."

He sat up in his chair. "Sure, Dan. What's up?"

"I'm working on the Wiederman deal today, and I have some questions about it."

Steve laughed sarcastically. "I'm not shocked. I just didn't expect anybody to pay any attention up there. They usually don't."

"What's going on, Steve?"

He suddenly got serious. "Dan, if I'm seen talking to you, and then something blows up, I'm history."

"I don't want to get you in trouble," I said. "I just want to do the right thing. If anybody gets in trouble, it'll be me, not you."

He stared at me for a moment. "Okay," he said finally, "here's the deal. The great new software for Wiederman doesn't work. It just plain doesn't work."

"But what about all the testing data that's in our presentation? What about our guarantees and promises of tech support?"

"It's bogus. Look, it all came down from Hogan. Last fall, he came in here and went ballistic all over Baker, yelling that he wanted this contract. Gerry told him that it couldn't be done by this spring, but you know how that goes over. Next thing I know, Hogan has Gerry in his office behind a closed door, and there's not a sound coming out of it. Hogan leaves. Then I see Baker come out as white as a sheet, and he tells us we've got to get it done, one way or another." Brunck stretched out his hands in exasperation.

"So, they've had us working under the gun for months now. But there hasn't been time to do it right. Wiederman's manufacturing and inventory controls are complicated, and their distribution is all over the map. We'd get some part of it working, then another part would go out of whack. Then we'd fix that one, and another would go haywire. The pressure was so great I started to lose my hair, and began to think seriously about seeing a shrink. And that's nothing compared to what Baker's been through. I think the man's about to have a heart attack."

Steven waited in silence as I digested his story. "So the software isn't going to work," I finally said thoughtfully.

"Not unless a miracle happens," Steven answered. "Look, you've got to get out of here before somebody sees you."

"Okay," I answered, "but do you have any documentation? Have you kept any records about what you've done?"

"You bet I have!" he said. "I'm not going to get caught with my pants down over this. I've worked like crazy, and I made sure my rear is covered. I put regular reports in writing to Baker, and I meticulously documented our progress … or, I should say, lack thereof." Brunck made a sour face and looked around. "I'll tell you what I'll do, Dan. You're okay, and I know I can trust you. I'll let you see a copy of my file on this deal. I keep another one at home, to be safe. Just keep it to yourself, okay? And give it right back as soon as possible."

"Right. Thanks a lot, Steve." I took the thick manilla folder from his hand and returned to my office.

Sitting again at my desk and before opening the folder, I picked up the phone and dialed Mary Lou Bernet's home number. No answer. Good. Maybe she's coming into the office this morning. I opened Steven's folder and began to read.

He had done a good job of documenting his activities. There were indeed meticulous reports about things they had tried and their results. I didn't comprehend much of the computer-speak, but I could tell generally what they were trying to do. There were a couple of dozen hard copies of detailed e-mails to Gerald Baker listing their progress. As the winter passed, there were more and more ominous warnings that bugs were not being worked out, along with discouraging prognostications about their ability to meet the deadline. There were also a half dozen memos from Baker to Brunck, flashing alternating hints of fear and anger, spurring them on to get it done. In the end, the conclusion was depressingly clear: the program was not nearly ready, and Steven held out little hope that his group could solve the problems anytime soon.

I closed the file. This is what I am supposed to sell? I am supposed to look Henry Wiederman, a fellow Christian, in the eye, and tell him a series of confident lies about our wonderful product and our ability to help him run his business through our technical know-how? And they are going to make me a half-partner for doing it. I remembered musing on the possibility of someday seeing "Hogan, Jeter, White & Mathewson" in print. Now it made my stomach turn. Why would I want my name linked with theirs?

"Lord Jesus, what am I going to do?" I prayed. "I can't go through with this, knowing what I know. But how am I going to get out of it? I can't directly use the information Steven gave me, because I promised him I'd keep it confidential. Lord, I'm trusting you to guide me."

I sat gazing out of the window for a few minutes, thinking calmly and quietly. Then I pulled out my Bible once more, and returned to the passage about the Bema. This time, I read the verses that preceded it:

> Therefore we are always confident and
> know that as long as we are at home in the
> body we are away from the Lord. We live
> by faith, not by sight. We are confident, I
> say, and would prefer to be away from the

body and at home with the Lord. (2 Corinthians 5:6-8)

Boy, did those verses have more meaning to me now!
Having "seen" heaven, whether by a mere dream or by a
divine vision, I agreed with the apostle: I would much
rather be with the Lord in the heavenlies than to continue
living in a world of such hypocrisy and lying. Then my
eyes caught the next verses:

> So we make it our goal to please him,
> whether we are at home in the body or
> away from it. For we must all appear be-
> fore the judgment seat of Christ, that each
> one may receive what is due him for the
> things done while in the body, whether
> good or bad. (2 Corinthians 5:9,10)

"We make it our goal to please him," Paul said. I continued to ponder that phrase. We can't earn salvation or
God's acceptance by our lives, but we can indeed please
him by how we live. That thought moved my heart now, as
it never had before. Sometime in my past studies I had noticed it, though, because there was a cross-reference next to
verse nine. I looked up the connecting passage:

> For the appeal we make does not spring
> from error or impure motives, nor are we
> trying to trick you. On the contrary, we
> speak as men approved by God to be en-
> trusted with the gospel. We are not trying

to please men but God, who tests our
hearts. (1 Thessalonians 2:3,4)

I knew Paul was here speaking of his own ministry of
preaching the gospel, but it seemed to have an eerie rele-
vance to my predicament. I was being tempted to use
trickery for impure motives, but I had the same decision
looming before me as the apostle. The question was:
Would I try to please men, or would I choose to please
God? All my life, it seems, I have tried to please men. How
much wrong has resulted from pursuing that foolish goal?
But now I can seek to be a man approved by God.

"Lord," I prayed, "Show me how I can walk through
this mine field and please you by my decisions."

I stared out the window for a while longer, and began
to have an idea about what I could do.

CHAPTER 25

❧

I picked up my portfolio for the Wiederman deal and put Steven's folder beneath it as I walked out of my office, heading back to the technical wing. I nearly detoured when I passed Mary Lou's office and saw her light on, but I knew I had to press on for the moment.

Entering the software department, I saw Mike Kennedy, one of the top technoids, getting a snack from a dispenser in their break room. "Mike," I said, "I'd like to talk to your team about the Wiederman software before I go to sell it. Can you get them together for a brief meeting in an hour?" He said yes, and I thanked him. Stopping at Steven Brunck's office, I asked loudly, "Can you meet in sixty minutes, Steve?" He nodded, with raised eyebrows, and said, "Sure." I reached under my portfolio and laid his folder back on his desk. Leaning in where I could not be seen, I whispered, "Thanks."

Now, for Mary Lou. I stopped at her doorway and knocked. She looked up, appearing tired but composed, and smiled weakly. "Do you mind if I come in?" I asked. "Not at all," she replied. I shut the door behind me and sat down before her desk.

"Mary Lou," I began, "I want to apologize to you." She started, as if she never expected to hear me say those words. "I've really acted like an idiot about this Wiederman deal. I've been insensitive and foolish. Instead of helping you with all the trouble you've had to deal with, I've only made things worse. I've increased the pressure on you, and I'm sorry. I am asking you to forgive me."

Mary Lou placed both of her palms on the desk, her eyes large in utter surprise. "Gee, Dan ... I don't know what to say. Sure ... sure I forgive you." She looked down, and there seemed to be tears welling up in her eyes. She took a deep breath.

"Would you tell me how Michael is? What's the latest? And, is there anything I can do to help?"

She began slowly and haltingly, then picked up steam. Mary Lou talked almost non-stop for twenty-five minutes, detailing the medical condition of her child, and the exhausting series of examinations and procedures they had been through. I had little to say, but merely listened and nodded. It was no longer a mystery why her performance had dropped off so. I wouldn't have done any better under the strain she and her husband had endured.

Finally she ran out of gas. Mary Lou smiled genuinely for the first time. "So there you have it," she said. "No—to get back to your question—I don't think there is anything you or anyone else can do to help."

"Well, here's one thing," I answered. "I can at least not add to the problem. As far as I'm concerned, Mary Lou, there is no more pressure on you from my direction. You can take as much time as you need to care for your husband and child. Take a leave of absence if you want. You can go today ... right now, if you need to."

"But what about the Wiederman deal?" she protested. "I've been out of action enough as it is, and I don't want to leave you holding the bag all by yourself."

I made a sour face. "*Forget* the Wiederman deal! It's only one deal. I can handle it, no problem. And there'll be many more. You have higher priorities to worry about."

Mary Lou cocked her head to the side, clearly not believing her ears. "I don't know what's happened to you, Dan, but you sound very different from the person who's been talking about nothing but Wiederman for six months."

I smiled and shrugged. "Like I said, Mary Lou, I was wrong and I'm sorry. I'd like to do things right from here on out."

"Well, I appreciate it, Dan. I'll keep doing the best I can, but I appreciate the freedom from pressure."

"You've got it, then. Don't worry about it anymore. If anybody else has a problem about what you're doing, I'll take care of it."

Mary Lou's relief was evident. I thought she would begin crying again, but this time from joy. There was one more issue I wanted to bring up, but I felt nervous about it. I decided to give it a shot.

"Mary Lou, there's one more thing I'd like to suggest, maybe one more way to get you some help." I paused, and she waited patiently. "I'm a little uncomfortable bringing this up, because it's a personal issue. But if you don't mind talking about it..." I paused again. She still waited. "I wonder if you and John have a church of your own. A place where people know you, and can give you some support?"

Mary Lou looked surprised, but not offended. "No, not really. I don't suppose I've been in a church since I was a little girl ... except for our wedding, that is."

"Well, here's why I think it's important," I continued. "First of all, a good church is like an extended family. There are people who know you, and who care about you. They'll pray for you, and help in many practical ways. I've seen other people in our church in situations as hard as yours, and you wouldn't believe how others stepped forward to help. I've seen them bring meals, provide transportation, and even clean people's homes. Not that they're perfect people, because they're not. I'm no great saint, either. But you can meet people who are really men and women of God, who can help you.

"Second, you can hear good teaching to help you deal with the stress you're under. Our pastor is gifted at taking the Bible and explaining it to regular people like you and me. The Bible is amazing. It talks about real life and real people. Jesus said that if we listen to his word, we'll know the truth and the truth will set us free. When you're under severe stress, like you and John are dealing with, it puts distance between you in your relationship, even if you love each other. It's like being a mountain climber or marathon runner. In those activities, your body is under severe stress and you've got to feed it major amounts of calories to keep it going. Your inner life is the same when you're under stress. You need spiritual calories to keep your inner life healthy. That's what a good time in Bible study does for you. Does that make sense?"

"Yes, I suppose it does," she answered. "The part about stress is sure true. John and I hardly talk to each other anymore. We're so tired and worn down all the time."

"That's what I'm talking about," I replied. "Now, you might have a church where you would rather go, but you don't live that far from Susan and me, so I'd like to invite you to ours. I really think you'd like it, if you give it a try."

Mary Lou expressed her interest, so I wrote down the directions and time of services for her. Before, I would have been extremely reluctant to be so direct, but for some reason I felt confident to forge ahead.

"There's just one more thing, Mary Lou. Though I really do believe a church would be a great help to you, that's not the most important issue. The most important thing is whether we have a personal relationship with God himself. I'm not presenting myself as some great spiritual man, but my relationship with Jesus Christ is the most important thing in my life. I haven't always lived like it. In fact, I've been a failure as a Christian many times. But it is still true. He is faithful, even if we are not. He is good, and he is powerful. If I were in your shoes, I don't think I could do it on my own. But the Bible says, 'I can do everything through him who gives me strength.'"

Mary Lou seemed to be listening intently. I went on. "So, I wonder. Has anyone ever explained this to you before? Do you think you understand what it means to be a Christian, or how someone could become one if they wished?"

"No," she answered thoughtfully. "I don't think I've ever thought about it much. I figured people either were church-goers or they weren't. I wasn't. So what does it mean to be a Christian, if it's not just a good person who goes to church?"

That was an open door if I'd ever heard one, so I went on to explain (haltingly and clumsily) the gospel to Mary

Lou. We talked for twenty-five more minutes, as I answered questions and drew diagrams. At the end of the time, she said that she understood the basics of the gospel and promised to think it over carefully. In closing, I wrote out John 3:16 on a note-card, and gave it to her. She thanked me profusely for the conversation, and I left.

"Thank you, Lord!" I prayed, as I returned to the technical wing. "Thank you that I had the chance to apologize to Mary Lou, and that she accepted it, and even more, that I was able to talk to her about you. Lord Jesus, please help her to see you, and draw her to yourself. Now, Lord, I need you to help *me*."

I took my seat at a conference table, along with six members of the technical team, Steven Brunck included. I had to find a way to get the conversation going in the right direction without giving away that Steven had fed me information.

"Thank you all for meeting with me," I began. "I know you have worked extremely hard on this project, and so have I. This afternoon, I am scheduled to meet with Henry Wiederman, so I want to make sure I understand all I need to know about our product." They all seemed understanding and agreeable, so I continued. "Why don't you give me a quick recap of what you learned along the way?"

Steven pointed to Mike Kennedy, so he began. I mainly listened and asked questions. All of my questions were reasonable in context and were quite proper in light of the looming deal, and so no confidence was broken with Steven. As the conversation progressed, I felt that God himself was guiding its course. Each explanation led to natural questions, which led to more information, which I could then naturally pursue. I was involved in silent prayer much of the time, seeking God's wisdom and trusting his promise to "make my paths straight." Several times, I did not really know what to say next, but a question would come to my mind that opened up a new line of inquiry. In the end, I was able to elicit by honest conversation and questioning the same conclusions I had gained by reading Steven's file.

"So," I concluded after ninety minutes, "let me see if I've got this right. You have surfaced about eight to ten major problems in developing this software package that remain unsolved. You think it might work, once it's tied into Wiederman's manufacturing and distributing operations, but nobody will commit to that beforehand. In fact, if you are being totally honest, all of you express grave doubts as to whether it will do half of what we are going to promise it will do. Is that right?"

The six team members looked around at one another in silence, then all focused on Steven. He began to nod slightly, and sighed. "That's about the size of it, Dan," he said.

"Then how did we ever get to this point?" I pressed. "How did all these contracts and specs get written up to be presented today?"

Clearly, nobody wanted to answer this question aloud. They just stared at me.

"How about if I hazard a guess?" I said. "Gerald told you to write it up, regardless of the real state of affairs." They just continued to stare at me. "Okay, ladies and gentlemen, thank you for your time." They all left quickly and in silence.

CHAPTER 26

Our department receptionist waved to attract my attention as I was walking back to my office. "Your wife has called twice this morning, and wants you to call her at work as soon as you can," she said.

I smiled to myself as I punched the number. That's just like her, I thought. My note has her curiosity working at warp speed.

"All right," Susan said after hearing my voice, "I've got the sitter. What's going on?" Her voice sounded friendly, but with a wary and suspicious edge.

"Nothing special," I answered, laughing. "Can't I ask my charming and beautiful wife out on a date without ulterior motives?"

"No, you can't," she answered. "There's something going on. Are you mad at me about anything?"

"No, I'm not mad at you! Honest!" I sighed and paused. "Okay. There are some things going on," I said, my tone changing from playful to serious, "but it's about work, not you." Susan waited in silence. "Honey, I really can't talk now. But there are some serious things going on I need to talk to you about. Can it wait till tonight?"

"Okay," she said. "I'll be ready."

Without replacing the receiver, I next dialed Gerald Baker's number. "Gerald," I said, "I need to talk to you. Are you free right now?" He answered affirmatively, and I walked over to his office.

"Gerald, we've got a problem, and we need to talk about it right now," I said without preliminaries.

"I should say *you* do have a problem," he answered emphatically. "I've heard already about your little meeting this morning. Do you have any idea what you're doing?"

"I think what I'm doing is finding out the truth about our product," I replied. "It's my job to sell our software and make deals. But to sell a product, I have to believe in it. It's perfectly proper for me to investigate the quality of our software so I know what I'm talking about to a customer. And what I've heard is disturbing."

"Not half as disturbing as what you're going to hear if you screw this thing up!" Baker said, blustering. "Mathewson, you're digging in areas where you're going to get hurt. And not only you. A lot of other people are going to get hurt, too, if you keep this up." Baker's face was reddening, and droplets of sweat were breaking out on his forehead.

"Gerald," I continued in a calmer voice, trying to slow down the conversation, "you are one of the best in the business at what you do. I respect you and your knowledge. It's because I have a high degree of confidence in you that I've been slow to ask these kinds of questions. I also

like you personally, and we've never had a problem working together. Don't you feel the same?"

Baker seemed to physically relax a little, and he sat back
in his chair. He took a deep breath. "Yeah, I do, Dan.
You've always been good to work with. That's why ..." He
couldn't seem to finish the sentence. He just shook his
head sadly.

"So, Gerald. Tell me the truth. How good is this software package? In your opinion, is it good? Is it going to
work?"

Gerald breathed deeply again. He looked down at his
desk, then he looked up and seemed to stare into space.
"No," he said eventually. "It isn't good. And no, it won't
work. I don't mean it won't do anything right. But it sure
won't do all that we'll represent it as doing. And it could
possibly be worse than that."

"What do you mean by 'worse than that'?" Baker said
nothing. Like my earlier conversation with the team, I was
being forced to draw my own conclusions, without his
having to voice them. I sat and thought for a moment.
"There's just one thing that occurs to me that would fit
into the category of 'worse than that.' This program could
crash ... could conceivably crash, and foul up
Wiederman's manufacturing and distributing systems. As
a result, they could default on their contracts, and we
could be hit with a major liability lawsuit. Is that what
you're thinking, Gerry?"

"Yes," he answered without feeling.

I sat in quiet thought for another few moments. My
emotions were screaming to ask, "Then why in the world
are you presenting it to me to sell?" But I felt so sorry for
the deflated figure sitting across from me that I couldn't

bear to deal him another blow. Instead I said, "All right, then. There's just one more question I want to ask you. Gerald, if you were in my place, would you go in to see Henry Wiederman today and try to sell him our package?"

Baker leaned forward with his elbows on his desk, and folded his hands in front of his face. He looked down and said nothing for a minute. Then, in a voice that seemed close to breaking, he said, "If I were you? Would I sell it?" More silence. Then, "No. I wouldn't. I wouldn't, Dan, if I were you." Baker looked at me steadily in the eyes, his own looking lifeless and beaten. I thanked him and left.

Sitting again in my own office, I thought about the one major hurdle left, and dreaded it. It was now up to me to talk to Derek Hogan about the deal. If ever I felt out on a limb alone, it was now. I started to get extremely angry. How come *I'm* the one holding the bag? I internally yelled. *I* didn't create this software! *I* didn't make all those promises, then deliver a substandard product! Now it's *my* income, and *my* livelihood, and *my* reputation that's going to get flushed down the drain!

I fumed in impotent anger for ten or fifteen minutes. With any less self-control, I would have begun flinging office furniture around or out the window. I slumped in my chair with my head in my hands. "Lord Jesus," I prayed, "what do I do now? I wish I could blame everybody else, but I've got my share of the blame, too. I was out there pushing for this deal like all the rest of them."

Once having begun to talk to the Lord about the situation, I could see some things clearly and honestly. I hate to admit it, but the angry face of Derek Hogan haunted my thoughts. Facing him was my great fear. We men are funny creatures. We don't mind admitting to problems with anger, but no man wants to admit being afraid. But it was the truth. I was afraid, and my anger was a mask, a secondary response to my fear. "Lord," I prayed again, "I am a frightened man. How do I deal with it?" Not knowing the answer, I picked up my Bible. After thumbing through it for several minutes, I came across a verse I had underlined sometime in the past:

> For God did not give us a spirit of timidity, but a spirit of power, of love and of self-discipline. (2 Timothy 1:7)

As I read that verse over and over again, it seemed as if my inner life was being fueled. "Lord Jesus, I am a man without a backbone," I prayed. "Over the years, I have been tested many times, and seldom have I chosen the right way. I want to this time, but I need you to give me the power. Your word here says that the fear I'm feeling did not come from you. That means it must have come from the pit of hell. It says the spirit you give is one of power and love and self-discipline, and do I need those! Father in heaven, let me be this kind of man."

Once again, I had written a note in the margin (praise God for those past times in Bible study!), and I was directed to another verse:

> Fear of man will prove to be a snare, but whoever trusts in the Lord is kept safe. (Proverbs 29:25)

That's the story of my life! I thought. All my life, I have lived as a slave to the opinions of men. "Lord God," I said, "forgive me for fearing men more than I feared you! Help me to see my life and this situation from your perspective, and help me to see you in the picture, so the opinions of people will not matter."

Closing the Bible and putting it back in the drawer, I stared out the window and took a deep breath. It was time to call on Derek Hogan.

I didn't have to. A human hurricane blew into my office. "Can you tell me what the hell is going on, and what the hell you're doing?" he shouted, slamming my office door.

I didn't like being shouted at, but neither was I as intimidated as I feared I would be. Though I felt relatively calm, I wasn't sure how to answer that question. "I'm not doing anything special, Derek, except trying to do my job properly."

"Doing your *job*?" he sneered. "Since when is it your *job* to be running around our offices, creating havoc, and jeopardizing our chances to make a major deal?"

"I'm not trying to jeopardize anything," I replied. "I've been simply asking our people about our product. The same product I'm supposed to sell to a customer. *They* are the ones telling me about the problems. How could I be expected to go tell a customer, face to face, about a product without complete understanding of what I was selling?" Strangely, instead of the fear I dreaded experiencing, I felt completely at ease. I believe it was simply the confidence that comes from believing you are right and telling the truth.

Hogan glared at me, his eyes the blackest I had ever seen. He then turned and stood looking out the window. A minute or two passed. Then he seemed to relax. He turned back to me and smiled. "Okay. I guess you're right, Mathewson." He shrugged, looking at me as if I were his best friend. "Come to think of it, of course you've got to look into our product. That's why I have such confidence in you as a deal maker. You do your homework."

I blinked in surprise. I didn't expect this.

"Sure," Hogan continued, "check it out. But be quick, will you? Find out whatever it is you want to know. No software is perfect, and we never claim it is. In fact, knowing where the bugs are is half the solution. So find out. But we've got less than three hours left before you have to talk to Wiederman. You'll be prepared, and I know you'll do the job. And then you can claim that little reward I placed on your desk Friday."

The half-partnership offer. There's a lot of money to be made. It's that far away, right there to be taken. And, yes, I have always tried to do my homework. A rush of pride swept up and down my spine. I do quality work! No other company could offer perfect software, either. So is it that big a deal?

The face of Henry Wiederman flashed into my mind. This man is my brother, I thought. One day he and I will watch each other's evaluation at the Bema, along with all the other Christian saints of history. And even if he weren't, there is still the issue of the facts I had learned. The technical team and Gerald Baker agreed: the software package will not work. I cannot sell it.

I shook my head slowly. "I'm sorry, Derek. I know that nobody can make perfect software, but it at least has to be safely usable. Our own tech people don't promise that it is. They can't even assure me that it won't blow up Wiederman's whole operation. It isn't in Wiederman's best interest to buy it, and, frankly, it isn't in the best interest of Hogan, Jeter, and White to sell it. When it comes down to it, if Henry Wiederman decides to buy our product, it will be because of his confidence in my word, and I can't offer it. I can't look him in the eye and advise him to buy what I'm selling."

Hogan looked like a volcano about to erupt. His chiseled features convulsed, his clear complexion became flushed, and his eyes burned brighter and brighter as I talked. He clenched both his fists.

"Do you mean to tell me," he exploded, "that you are going to do this *now*? After all the months this company has poured into this project, you are going to throw it out the window *now*?" He looked as if he would either pull a gun and shoot me, or drop dead of a heart attack right on my desk.

"I'm truly sorry, Derek, that it has to be now. Maybe I have been wrong. Maybe I have been lax about checking into these things before. We were all working at such high intensity that maybe we failed to stop and ask these questions before, when we should have. But it is never too late to do the right thing. Today, the right thing is to pull the plug. It would not be right to sell a fraudulent product."

"*Do the right thing? Do the right thing?*" Hogan was so furious, I wouldn't have been surprised if he punched me in the face. "Who are *you* to tell me about the right thing? Who the hell do you think you are? Who do you think you are, you little slug, to use a word like 'fraudulent'? Do *you* want to take on our legal department? Is *that* what you want?"

"Derek, none of this is what I want. I want to work hard, I want to make a good living for my family, I want to give you, my employer, my best, honest effort. But I want it to be an honest effort. That's why I can't represent us in this deal."

Hogan's appearance and voice changed. He was no longer furious, red-faced, and loud. He became deathly cold and quiet. He nearly whispered his words. "Your days of making a good living are over, Mathewson. If you bail out of this, I'll ruin you. You not only won't work here, I'll make sure you don't work *anywhere* in this business! You'll be finished. Give me that partnership agreement."

I handed over the package he had given me on Friday, his personalized sticky note still attached. Hogan took it in his two hands, and tore it twice. He flung the pieces to the corners of my office. "*That's* your career, Mathewson. You want to make an honest living? Fine. Do manual labor. Become a schoolteacher. Dig ditches. Flip burgers. You won't be seeing the kind of money you could have seen here. *Never again!*" Hogan turned on his heels and left my office, slamming the door behind him.

Chapter 27

$\backsim$

I felt shell-shocked, not sure what to do next. Now that the worst had happened, the confrontation was not really all that bad. But I knew enough about Derek Hogan to know that the real "worst" was still ahead. Unlike many of the typical blowhards you meet in the world, when Derek Hogan says he'll ruin somebody, he means it and he can do it.

"Lord, what am I going to do for a living, if he goes through with his threat? Professionally speaking, he definitely can ruin me. He can fix it so I can hardly work anywhere in this town."

Instead of the sharp, paralyzing fear I was tempted to feel earlier, I felt the cold, humbling kind of fear you experience when you know a King Kong-sized difficulty lies dead ahead. It was a jaw-setting, eye-dimming foreboding, like that of a soldier about to enter a desperate battle, or someone who learns he or she has cancer and anticipates many months or years of treatment and surgery. I knew that in a few short hours, my life had taken a sharp detour onto a very dark road. In a few short minutes, I had made irrevocable decisions. My life and future had become a huge unknown.

Without much conscious thought I did what was rapidly becoming a habit: when in doubt, reach for the Bible. Looking for help in the area of money and income, I found this passage:

> Keep your lives free from the love of money and be content with what you have, because God has said, "Never will I leave you; never will I forsake you." So we say with confidence, "The Lord is my helper; I will not be afraid. What can man do to me?" (Hebrews 13:5,6)

Those words brought unspeakable comfort. My security was not in my ability to generate income, or in my working in any particular job. My security was in the faithfulness of God, who had promised never to leave or forsake me.

How different from Hogan's philosophy! "Bucks is the name of the game," he always said. No, it's not! I inwardly asserted. Bucks is *not* the name of *my* game. "Lord Jesus, knowing *you* is the most important thing, and I want my life to be pleasing and useful to you."

Ninety minutes later, I was sitting in the office of Henry Wiederman. He was surprised and irritated that I requested an immediate audience rather than the meeting we had scheduled, but he agreed to meet with me. Wiederman was a gruff-looking, blunt-speaking septuagenarian, and he scared many people. But I had known him for years, and knew him to be kind and generous inside. Henry Wiederman was a good man, and a sincere Christian.

He wasn't, however, very pleased that Hogan, Jeter & White was not going to meet the agreed-upon deadline to present our completed software package.

"What's the matter with you people, Dan?" he groused. "We've put all kinds of development on hold, waiting for this. I've been counting on you."

"Yes, sir," I agreed. "I'm as sorry as I can be. I know we have let you down. Our people have given it their best effort. They've really tried. But as of this date, we don't have a product I can confidently offer to you, and I won't bring you something I don't believe in myself."

Henry snorted impatiently, and looked away for a few moments. He seemed to be speaking half to himself. "I suppose we'll have to go back to Mischell and Associates. They nearly beat you out in the beginning to get a shot at this deal. Frankly, Dan," he said, looking back at me, "it was really because of you that I decided to give Hogan the job in the first place. I'm really disappointed in you."

"Yes, sir. To be perfectly honest, I'm very disappointed in myself, too."

Henry snorted again, and stared me in the face for a minute. I simply waited, submitting to whatever would follow. At last, he seemed to soften. "All right, Dan," he said, in a more gentle voice, "nobody hits a home run every time up. I'm sure you gave it your best effort. Maybe next time."

I thanked him, again apologizing for our failure to come through, shook his hand and left.

The offices of Hogan, Jeter & White were as quiet as a
tomb when I returned. I don't know if people were deliberately avoiding me, or if it was just my self-consciousness
that made it seem so. But walking down the hallways and
past the work areas and offices, it seemed that people were
too preoccupied with work or conversations to notice me.
Those that did offered only a quick wave or lame smile. I
found it impossible not to believe that word had gotten
around of my actions and the confrontation with Hogan.
My career as a non-person has begun, I thought. I don't
believe I ever felt so alone in my life, in terms of human
companionship. And yet, I felt that Jesus Christ was with
me every moment.

I sat in my office and tried to work. There was a fat
folder on my desk containing other deals and projects going on in the office. I opened it and tried to concentrate,
but found it impossible. A voice kept hammering away at
the back of my mind: *What are you doing this for? You're
wasting your time. Your career is over at this place.*

I shook my head, trying to clear it. "I don't believe it," I
contended. "Lord Jesus, I don't know what the future
holds for me, but I know you, and I believe in you. I believe that you will never leave me nor forsake me, and I believe you'll guide me."

Is it time to go home yet? I checked my watch. Rats! It's
only three. Too early to go home. But I may as well leave. I
felt too restless and distracted to work effectively, so I
grabbed my Bible and briefcase, and left. Nobody seemed
to notice.

It would have been nice to see Joe Thesecurityguard in
the lobby. I would have enjoyed a brief conversation, but it
was long past his quitting time. I got into my car and began

driving north. I remembered that Franky's deli was just another exit ahead, and I decided to stop in. It would be a good place to park my body for a little while.

As I neared the exit, I looked at the blue sky dotted with small white clouds. Feeling a little silly, I peered upward, hoping to see a door opening in the heavens. No. Not today. "Lord," I said, "if you did decide to come today, it would be all right with me!" But the traffic continued moving as usual.

I ordered a chocolate milkshake and sat alone by the big picture window. I can't say exactly what I thought about for almost two hours. My mind was so tired from the events of the day, that I probably didn't think about much at all. Once or twice, I nearly shed tears, just from feeling overwhelmed. But never did I feel any regrets. I had done the right thing.

Eventually I found my way home, arriving much earlier than usual. Mark was kicking a soccer ball in the front yard. When he saw me, he ran to me wearing a happy grin and threw his arms around my neck. It was the best thing that had happened to me all day. Janie and Jeffrey also gave me tight hugs, which felt like a million dollars. Susan smiled and was friendly, but I knew she was itching to know what was happening. I have to say that she was about the most beautiful and welcome sight these mortal eyes have ever seen.

Before too long, we were seated together at our favorite local restaurant, a small Italian place. In a secluded, darkened booth, we ordered. Then Susan blurted out in a stage whisper, "All right! I've been going crazy all day. What is the big news?"

Omitting any mention of my dream (I didn't want her to think I was losing my mind), I told Susan in complete detail what had happened that day. I told her of vague and disturbing feelings regarding the Wiederman deal that had been building up, and of how I decided to investigate. I described my meetings with the technical team and with Gerald Baker, and the confrontation with Derek Hogan. Finally, I told of my meeting with Henry Wiederman. Our salads came and went, our main courses came and went, and still I talked, factually and unemotionally. Finally, the entire story had been told.

Susan seemed to stare over my shoulder. She had said little during the entire time, but never appeared bored. She had been listening carefully.

"So," she said quietly, after a time. "Are you telling me that you walked away from thousands and thousands of dollars today, maybe millions?" She screwed up her face in a squint and peered into my eyes. "Are you saying that you may have thrown your career away because you didn't believe in your company's product? And that you told Derek Hogan to his face that you would not sell his product, because you thought it would be dishonest to do so?"

She was waiting for an answer. "Yes," I said.

"Why would you do that?"

That's a question I really didn't know how to answer properly. I didn't want to sound trite or pious, but I didn't want to look foolish, either. "Susan, I've been a Christian since I was about twelve, but I've been a pretty poor one. I had my fire insurance policy, as we used to say, and I knew I was going to heaven when I died, but I didn't relate it much to how I lived here and now. But lately, I've been thinking a lot about the Lord and about what he must think of me. I've been studying the Bible a little more, and I've been seeing things more from God's standpoint. I began to realize how many lies I've fallen into believing, and how many stupid things I've done because my eyes were on the wrong things. I'm not claiming to be some kind of spiritual giant or anything, but I don't want to live that way anymore. I just don't want to be that kind of person anymore. One of these days, I ... all of us ... will stand face to face with Jesus Christ, and he will call for an accounting of our stewardship on earth. I don't understand for sure what heavenly rewards are all about, and I'm not really motivated by the thought of jewels in my crown. But I do know this: I want to hear the Lord say to me, 'Well done, good and faithful servant.' And while I'm here on earth I want to live a life pleasing and useful to him. I want to get back to enjoying my relationship with him and experiencing his life now, not just some future day."

I didn't mean to preach, but once I got started, I kept speaking with real feeling.

Susan looked at me without expression for a few more moments. Then she said again in that quiet voice, "So you are saying that you've done these things because you want to be a better Christian? Because you really want to take seriously the kind of life God wants you to live?"

"Yes," I said.

Susan looked like she might cry. "I've never been prouder of you than I am right now."

I thought I might begin crying. Until she said it, I didn't realize how apprehensive I felt about how she would respond. Part of me feared that she would hit the ceiling at the news, and leave me.

I choked a little on the words I began to say next. "I'm so glad to hear to you say that. But, Susan, you realize that this means a lot of trouble for us? Life is going to get hard."

"Of course," she said matter-of-factly. "We'll have to move to a much smaller house, and strip down to as few bills as possible." She stared into space as she brain-stormed. "And I'll have to work more hours for a while. That'll be great with our owners. They've been after me to take on the senior management of the store for months, but I've been fighting them off. It's obviously one way the Lord intends to provide for us for a while." Susan scratched on the tablecloth with her fingernail, doing imaginary sums.

"But aren't you at all upset?" I asked her in my surprise. "Won't you be sorry to lose our dream house and have to move to a cheaper neighborhood?"

She didn't exactly say, "Pshaw," but the sound she made meant the same thing. "Daniel Mathewson, don't you know that I love *you*? I don't love our *house*. Sure, I like living well, but you and our children are the most important things in my life. *Things* don't mean anything! I can't think of anything that could make me happier than having a husband who truly wants to be a man of God.

"And, besides," she continued after a moment, "it will be worth every penny we lose to be out from under the influence of Derek Hogan!"

I was completely surprised by that sentiment. "You've never said anything like that before."

"You haven't been listening," she corrected me. "No, I never said it so bluntly before, but I've made it clear what I think of that man. He's a snake. He's evil. I've prayed for you for months, years, that you would see the truth and get away before it's too late."

"What do you mean, 'before it's too late'?"

"I don't know for sure," Susan answered, "but mark my words: sooner or later that man will go down and take a lot of others with him. I was just terrified that you would be one of them."

"Well, remember," I said, "I haven't actually left yet. In spite of what happened today, I still work there."

She shook her head confidently. "It's just a matter of time. There's no way Hogan will put up with being crossed. There's no way he'll put up with having an honest man in his organization, because then he won't be able to control you. And anybody he can't control, he'll get rid of. You watch. It's just a matter of time!"

The dogmatism of Susan's outlook surprised me, but I had found her to be intuitively accurate before. "Whatever," I shrugged. "I don't know the future, and my performance in the past doesn't make me feel confident about myself. I just want to trust the Lord and walk ahead, one day at a time, and trust him to lead and provide. If you're with me, that's all I care about at this point."

"There's no *if* about it," she said.

I took her hand across the table. "I'm really thankful to have you," I said.

Susan just sat there, smiling, and looking beautiful.

EPILOGUE

꜀

About eighteen months have passed since the events of which I last wrote. That year and a half turned out to be the worst period of my adult life. It was extremely hard, both on me and on Susan. But we've stuck together, and I think we have grown closer and more mature. That year and a half also turned out to be the best period of my adult life. I have come to know and love Jesus Christ more deeply than I ever thought possible, and he has proven completely faithful, beyond my imagination.

Susan was right about Hogan. From the day I fouled up his plan, I became a non-person at Hogan, Jeter & White. I continued to work hard, but they made it impossible for me to continue. Hogan maneuvered things so that I was frozen out of any deal that might produce income for me. After my first year, I had negotiated a new contract where I worked on almost a straight commission basis, so that couldn't continue for very long.

The social atmosphere at the company was very hard to deal with, too. Those who were in the power circles turned their backs on me immediately, and said almost nothing to me apart from sarcastic digs. Even the good people there, who had always been friendly before, withdrew. It was mostly from fear, I think. It had been made clear that I was *persona non grata*, and anyone would have paid a price for appearing to befriend me. I didn't really blame them, so I held no grudges. Where I had once been *in*, which I had wanted so desperately, I was now clearly *out*. But I couldn't have cared any less. Having seen the inner circle for what it was, I was more than willing to be an outsider. You can't escape, however, the practical need for an income, so after sticking it out for about three months, I gave my notice.

Hogan had clearly been looking forward to this day. "So," he said with a smile, "you're ready to go out into the world and try your wings. I hope you enjoy it out there."

I tried to retain some measure of dignity. "Derek, I've learned a lot from working here, and I want to thank you for the opportunity. I think it's time for me to try something else."

"Yes, speaking of that," he said, pulling out a stack of papers, "I'm sure you remember the non-compete contract you signed when you started here. Unlike the casual verbal agreements you like to work by, we prefer to do things in a businesslike manner."

Judging by Hogan's appearance, I don't think a prime steak would have tasted as good as the words he was speaking. His eyes were bright with excitement.

"I'm sure," he continued, "that I don't need to remind someone like you, someone of such evident integrity, but here's what you agreed to. For five years you won't work in any type of software creation business. Nor will you work for any firm that competes with Hogan, Jeter, and White in any way. Now, if you like, I'm sure Mr. Edwin White and his associates will be glad to explain the contract to you."

I wasn't ready for that blow, having forgotten the details of my contract. What could I have been thinking when I signed that? It's absurd! No business makes people sign ridiculous agreements like that! At least, not people on my level. Sometimes company founders have to sign five year non-compete covenants. Sometimes senior partners or head software designers do, too, but not mid-level managers or brokers. What have I done?

"Oh, of course, there is one way you might get out of it," Hogan continued. "All this will be null and void if Hogan, Jeter, and White should go into bankruptcy." He smiled again, revealing his perfect set of perfectly white teeth.

Right. That's likely to happen! I said good-bye and left.

So began what I have taken to calling "my wilderness wanderings." Thankfully, Susan and I had already begun preparations. We had sold our house, jettisoning the huge payments, and had bought a much more modest home. She did step up her work commitment, which pained us both, but she asserted that for a brief period of our lives it would be a good idea. I had no choice but to agree. Susan turned out to be a real trooper, and if I ever have to go to war, she's the sidekick I want with me.

There were also occasional unforeseen blessings. One afternoon, Jeffrey burst through the door of our home. "Mom! Mom!" he yelled. "Do we have any balloons? I need to make some water balloons! We're going to have a water balloon war!" As Susan good-naturedly went looking for balloons, Jeffrey came over to my easy chair. "Dad," he said, "this is the best place we ever lived!"

I was surprised, since this home was worth a quarter of the one we had left. "Why do you think that?" I asked.

"Because it's fun!" Jeffrey exclaimed. "We have lots of kids who live here, and all our houses are right next to each other. There's always somebody to play with." Susan called him over to the sink, and they began filling balloons.

Seven year-olds look at things differently than adults, I thought. And they sometimes have more sense about what is important. Watching the children, I decided he was right. Our children actually did enjoy living in our new economy home much more than the upscale one.

I'd be lying if I implied it was easy. We have both shed tears, though mainly alone or with friends, so that we wouldn't needlessly burden one other. I leaned on John Lancaster, one of the pastors at our church. Early in the process, I asked him to meet with me for breakfast, where I told him the whole story. He proved to be a great friend, offering constant encouragement and support, and practical help as well. John got me connected again with the body of Christ, and I have made a whole set of close friends from guys at church. We have a group that meets weekly for an early breakfast at a local restaurant, where we study, talk, and pray together. That group became my life-line (beyond my relationship with the Lord himself).

John Lancaster is also the only person on earth to whom I have told the story of my dream. He listened to the whole thing patiently, then thought about it for a while before responding.

"It sounds theologically accurate, so far as it goes … as far as I can imagine, anyway," he said. "I certainly have no idea what the judgment at the Bema will look like or how it will proceed, but those are some interesting ideas in your dream. I'm not qualified to say one way or another whether you have had a vision of heaven. From what I know of your background and experiences, it could be explained in natural terms as an ordinary dream. Though you admit that you strayed for a while from the Bible, you had done enough study in your past to account for the knowledge you showed. Plus, you told me that you've read a couple of books on church history, so that part of the dream is explainable, too. So the answer is, I don't know."

I was disappointed, hoping to find out the answer to this mystery regarding a dream that changed the course of my life.

John went on. "To tell you the truth, Dan, it isn't important. What's the difference? By far the most important thing is that God used it to get you back on the right track. Just stay on the right track, and one of these days we'll all know what the Bema will be like."

That's pretty much how it still stands. I don't think I'll ever know any more in this world. It was John's idea that I write down the dream and my story. "It'll help you remember all the details," he said. "And, you'll never know how encouraging your story might be to yourself in some future day, or to someone else." So I have taken his suggestion.

With the restrictions in my non-compete agreement, I was severely limited in what I could do for income. I discovered what the depths of depression and despair could be like as I struggled to find work. For a time, I simply tried to work anywhere, and sometimes had two or three part-time jobs going. I drove for a courier service. I worked for a while with a fellow church member who had a roofing business. I discovered how hot and hard that type of labor is, but actually kind of enjoyed it as a real change of pace from office work. I needed more steady income, though, and kept looking, but without success.

I think I hit the bottom of the barrel the day I applied to work for a local office supply company at minimum wage. The owner turned me down, because I was "vastly overqualified."

Returning to my car, I sat for half an hour, alternately weeping and laughing. Here I was: a man who had not that long ago made a six-figure annual income. And I'd been turned down for a job at minimum wage! It was heart-breaking and hilarious at the same time.

Thankfully, Susan and I had savings to lean on, but we also knew we couldn't simply drain our accounts. Things started to get better. I eventually began working with another man I knew from church in his small computer hardware business. I didn't think I was technically strong enough to work in the hardware end, but I've done all right.

One of the most important things I did was to go back to see John Mischell. I confessed to him the wrong I had done in violating our agreement. I admitted without varnish how foolish and sinful I had been because of my ambition, and I asked him to forgive me. John rose from his chair and embraced me tightly, with tears in his eyes. He received me back graciously like the prodigal son. We were reconciled, and our friendship was more than restored. In fact, John gave me some business leads and endorsed me to others, which helped me get off the ground.

Having begun to make a steady living, I was also able to do something I had wanted to do for several months. The Bible warns that we should "not let our left hand know what our right hand is doing," so I don't want to trumpet a good deed. But with the help of John Mischell and a few other sincere believers of means, I was able to make sure that Gloria Perez got her wish. As long as she maintains a "B" average, Juanita's daughter will receive a fully funded college education from Tech.

For many months, my desert experience was a dark walk. In fact, while I never lost the consciousness that I was following the Lord's guidance faithfully, it felt as if life got darker and darker. One day it occurred to me: that is the way it would be for one walking through a dark forest. It would get progressively darker until you are halfway through, then it would begin to get lighter. The thought gave me hope, and it proved to be accurate. Susan and I stuck together, in spite of the stress and discouragement. We leaned on God and his Word, on one another, and on the people of God at our church. I actually found it harder to learn to receive as a needy person than it was to learn to give out of abundance. It was extremely humbling to be in a position of needing others, but it is healthy in the long run. We are, after all, completely dependent creatures, in spite of the self-sufficient arrogance to which we are prone. God uses our times of neediness to remind us that only he is completely self-sufficient.

This brings me to the amazing events of yesterday.

It was shortly after noon, and I was working quietly in the home office I had made out of our dining room. There was a knock at the front door, which Susan answered. Then I heard a man's voice, emotional and trembling, asking for me. It was Gerald Baker.

I was shocked at his appearance. He was disheveled and unshaven. He face appeared much older, and there was a wild look in his eyes.

"Dan, you've got to help me!" he said as he approached.

"Of course, Gerald," I said. "Sit down here."

"I'll get you something to drink," said Susan, giving me a questioning look as she headed for the kitchen.

"What's going on?" I asked, drawing up a chair.

"It's all hitting the fan, it's all hitting the fan," Baker said. "I'm in real trouble, Dan. I need help. But I don't know what anybody can do."

"Okay, Gerry," I said, trying to calm him. "Just tell me what is going on."

Baker wiped the sweat from his brow, and accepted a cold soft drink from Susan. He looked around in some exasperation, but seemed to calm down a little as he took a few sips. "You're the only one I could think of to talk to," he said. "I think I'm going to jail."

"To jail?" I exclaimed. "Why would you go to jail?"

"It's Hogan. You know how he does it. Dan, do you remember the Richardson deal a couple of years ago?"

"Yeah, sure," I answered. I remembered it well, though I hadn't had anything to do with it. "It was a big one, and a tough one, too."

"Tough is an understatement," Gerald said. "Hogan was all over me to get it done in time. I told him it couldn't be done, but he offered me big bucks to pull it off." Baker slapped the arm of his chair, and nearly sobbed, "I pulled it off all right!"

"Gerry, what did you do?"

After getting control of himself, he said plainly, looking me in the eye, "I stole it. I plagiarized part of the software. It was the only way to get it done by the deadline. Now they're going to find out. There are investigators in the office." Baker leaned forward with amazement in his eyes. "I think they're even looking at Hogan!" he hissed. "Not for the Richardson deal, but other things! It won't surprise you to hear he's done other things. I knew he skirted the line, but I always figured he was too smart to get caught. I think he's going down. And if he does, some other people are going with him! It might even bankrupt the company."

I was utterly astonished. Susan, who had sat down to listen, looked at me with wide eyes and open mouth, shaking her head.

"Dan," Baker continued, "you are so lucky you got out when you did. You're one of the few who won't be touched by this. I guess 'lucky' isn't the right word. It's because you were honest. And I want to say I'm sorry. I nearly roped you into trouble with the Wiederman deal. It was Hogan again. He threatened me. He told me he would see me in prison because of the plagiarized software if I didn't push the Wiederman software through, ready or not. I'm sorry, Dan, and I'm glad you didn't fall for it."

"I appreciate what you're saying, Gerry, but it's okay. I didn't get hurt. But what can I do for you?"

"I don't think anyone can help me," he said sadly. "I'm guilty and they're going to get me. But tell me." He looked at me with watery, imploring eyes. "You've always been a good man, an honest man. What can I do to get through this? What can I do just so I can sleep at night?"

"Gerald, I *haven't* always been an honest man. But I think I do know some things that can help you."

With half of my mind shouting, "Lord, I can't believe this is happening!" I began to tell Gerald about Jesus Christ. He responded like a man lapping up cold water after a walk through the desert, and we proceeded to talk for four hours. In the course of the conversation, he prayed with me, asking the Lord Jesus to come into his life and save him. We then went through the Bible, and I pointed out many passages upon which he could lean in the difficult days ahead. Before he left, he hugged me and Susan, and thanked us many times as tears streamed down his cheeks.

No spectacular miracle could have amazed Susan and me as much as the events of that afternoon. We talked late into the evening about the path we had walked, and expressed wonder at the way God had shielded me. I now could see what that partnership offer was all about. Hogan was not only using me to win over Henry Wiederman. He was also trying to rope me in as he did Baker and many others, where I would be compromised and brought under his power. My signature would have been on a lucrative partnership contract dated on Friday, before making a deal to sell defective software on Monday. There would have been a clear monetary motive for fraud. I would have become Hogan's slave, and possibly a candidate for jail, too.

Susan and I offered many prayers of thanks to God for his protection.

I think we both began to realize that we were healing. We were coming out again into the light. The Lord had been faithful to provide for us, financially, spiritually, and emotionally. We felt encouraged and reenergized to continue our walk of faith.

The Lord Jesus Christ has never meant more to me than he does right now. I haven't become righteous overnight. In fact, though I sincerely desire to be a man of God, I have only begun to learn how far short I fall of true righteousness. It's only as I began to grow that I learned how shallow I was before. I finally learned that spiritual depth is not measured by planting your body in a church building or through passing acquaintance with a few Bible verses. I've learned that the genuine Christian life is not hard; it is impossible. All I can do is to submit myself to the Lord, regularly expose myself to the truth of his Word, and live dependently—that is, by faith—one day at a time. Jesus Christ does the building, the molding, and the maturing. And he will one day evaluate the results. My greatest ambition continues to be to hear from his lips: "Well done, good and faithful servant." I choose to live for *The Day* rather than for *today*. And in that day, I want to have a crown to throw at his feet.

I often wonder if there is a Uriel watching over me and strengthening me, but, of course, he wouldn't be allowed to make his personal presence known. I hope I'm making his job a little easier than I used to.

I frequently find myself looking toward the sky, longing to hear a trumpet sound, hoping to see a rich golden light that one can taste as well as see. I would love to discover that time was being pierced by eternity, and see the Bridegroom coming for his bride. Maybe today.

When the risen, glorified Christ gave his revelation of the future to the apostle John, he finished by saying, "Yes, I am coming soon."

Amen. Come, Lord Jesus!